Miracleville

Miracleville

MONIQUE POLAK

ORCA BOOK PUBLISHERS

Library and Archives Canada Cataloguing in Publication

Polak, Monique
Miracleville / Monique Polak.

Issued also in electronic format.
ISBN 978-1-55469-330-6

I. Title.
PS8631.043M57 2011   JC813'.6   C2010-908042-4

First published in the United States, 2011
Library of Congress Control Number: 2010942082

Summary: Ani's faith is tested when her mother is paralyzed, her younger sister
starts having sex and questions arise about the identity of Ani's father.

*Orca Book Publishers is dedicated to preserving the environment and has printed
this book on paper certified by the Forest Stewardship Council.*

Orca Book Publishers gratefully acknowledges the support for its publishing programs
provided by the following agencies: the Government of Canada through the Canada Book
Fund and the Canada Council for the Arts, and the Province of British Columbia
through the BC Arts Council and the Book Publishing Tax Credit.

Cover design by Teresa Bubela
Typesetting by Nadja Penaluna
Cover photo by Getty Images
Author photo by Monique Dykstra

ORCA BOOK PUBLISHERS
PO Box 5626, Stn. B
Victoria, BC Canada
V8R 6S4

ORCA BOOK PUBLISHERS
PO Box 468
Custer, WA USA
98240-0468

www.orcabook.com
Printed and bound in Canada.

14 13 12 11 • 4 3 2 1

For my sister Carolyn, who understands
that miracles are possible

One

C olette drags one foot along the floor. "Please, *mademoiselle*," she says, grabbing my elbow. "I know you're closing up, but I need a bottle of Saint Anne's Miracle Oil. A little of your oil and I'll be dancing again. I was a ballerina"—her voice cracks—"until a terrible thing happened. I was dancing in Paris, when a gray mouse ran across the stage. I tripped and...my career was ruined!"

Colette covers her mouth and sobs. Loudly.

"Stop it!" I tell Colette as I spray the front window with cleaning solution. This stuff might be eco-friendly, but it leaves pale streaks on the glass. "It isn't right to make fun of the pilgrims," I say. "They're our best customers."

"*They're our best customers*," Colette mimics me in a shrill voice.

I grit my teeth. I hope I don't really sound like that.

Colette crosses her hands over her crotch and looks down at the floor. "Oh, I almost forgot—Saint Ani doesn't approve of imitations."

Mom and Dad named me for Saint Anne, and all my life I have tried my best to live up to the Blessed Saint's example. Saint Anne was patient; she never complained, even when she and her husband Joachim couldn't have a child. Saint Anne was kind; she never stopped loving Joachim even when he ran off to the desert in a snit. And Saint Anne was good. When she finally had a child—Mary—Saint Anne remembered her promise to God: that she would consecrate her child to Him. Which turned out to be a wise move since Mary ended up giving birth to Jesus, and where would we Catholics be without Him?

I want to be patient and kind and good too. But it's hard when Colette is acting so dumb. And not helping with the cleanup either. I swear she acts dumb on purpose.

I take a deep breath and spray the window again. Though the two of us are only eleven months apart, I'm the big sister. Colette's role model. But not a saint.

Outside, people are still milling around on Avenue Royale, the main street in our little town of Ste-Anne-de-Beaupré. Avenue Royale's so narrow there's only room for a sidewalk on one side. And the houses here in the center of town are set so close to the road that few have front lawns, just little patches of brown grass, and sometimes not even that.

In almost every group of people on the sidewalk, someone's in a wheelchair or hobbling on crutches. I look away. I know I should make an extra effort to show compassion for people who are handicapped, but sometimes the sight of a lolling head or a leg that ends in a stump makes me feel, to be honest, a little nauseated.

Each of those poor souls has come to Ste-Anne-de-Beaupré to pray for a miracle. Sometimes, when I'm walking on Avenue Royale, I feel hope hanging in the air like a living thing.

Every summer, religious pilgrims from around the world come to pray for Saint Anne's help and to buy souvenirs from the row of shops like ours on Avenue Royale. Saint Anne is one of Quebec's patron saints. Dad calls her the patron saint of lost causes. "Think of all the crippled people who come here," he says, rolling his eyes. "Have you ever seen a single one miraculously cured?"

Mom hates when Dad talks like that. "What about all those crutches hanging on the basilica walls? Every single pair was left behind by someone who didn't need them anymore! Besides," she tells Dad, "if you don't believe in miracles, they'll never happen."

"In all my life, I only ever witnessed one miracle," Dad likes to say to Mom. "And that was when a babe like you fell for a goofball like me."

"The world's sweetest goofball," Mom'll say.

I want to believe in miracles, really I do, but Dad's got a point. I've heard of miraculous healings, but I've never seen one. Then again, Mom's got a point too. Maybe if I believed more strongly, miracles would happen.

I know from Colette's grin that she's about to do another imitation. She doesn't know when to stop. Now she grabs a bottle of Saint Anne's oil from the shelf and studies the fine print on the label. "What's this?" She throws her hands up in the air. "*Avoid superstitious feelings*? *No guaranteed results*? And you're charging two dollars for this?" She takes a pretend swig. Then she does a pirouette on the faded wood floor in front of the cash register.

"Your oil," she cries out, "it's cured me! I can return to Paris and get even with that evil mouse!"

I pull down the window shade—a little too hard—and start dusting the Jesus snow globes. The Jesuses

4

inside give me mournful looks. Maybe they're cold in there or maybe they understand how hard it is to have a sister like Colette.

The truth is, I don't always feel like being good. Sometimes I want to scream. Or whack someone, usually Colette.

I make myself concentrate on the snow globes. One is covered with greasy fingerprints. When I pick it up, snow lands on Jesus' sinewy shoulders.

Colette grabs a *Bless This Trailer* plaque from the display case. "*Mademoiselle,*" she asks, "how much for this magnificent glow-in-the-dark plaque? My family and I are staying at the trailer park across the highway. The Lord is sure to visit a trailer with such a magnificent plaque outside."

"Enough!" I say as I attack the smudged snow globe with cleaning solution. For a moment, the sour smell of vinegar fills the shop.

But now Colette is rotating her lower arms in small circles as if she's in a wheelchair and is motoring down the shop's long center aisle. "Excuse me, *mademoiselle—*"

I march past Colette to the counter and grab the feather duster from the shelf under the cash register. I hum as I dust the Saint Anne nightlights. Dust particles rise into the air and then disappear.

Colette sighs. Maybe she'll quit fooling around if I ignore her. But the next second she's pressing her face up against mine. "*Mademoiselle*," she says, her dark eyes dancing, "please sell me a holy key chain. You see, my wife and I"—she turns to plant an airy kiss on the imaginary wife's cheek—"are trying to conceive, but the Lord has not yet blessed us with a child."

I'm still trying to ignore her when Colette reaches between her legs and tugs on an imaginary penis. I can feel my earlobes heat up. I don't know how Colette can make jokes about penises!

"It seems to work okay, doesn't it, my dear?" Colette asks, leering at the imaginary wife.

"Colette!" Though my voice is stern, I feel the corners of my mouth rise a little. I try to swallow my laughter, but it comes bubbling up. I'm laughing because Colette is being so outrageous, but also because I'm embarrassed. The feather duster falls to the floor, looking like the messy tail end of a chicken.

"Aha! I made you laugh!" Colette says, picking up the feather duster and swatting me with it.

From outside, we hear the singsong sound of Mom's voice. "It's lovely to see you too," she is saying to someone on the curb.

Colette lifts the window shade. "Who's that guy with Mom?"

I go to the window too.

The man has thick dark hair. When he turns his head, I notice his starched black collar and the white rectangular tab at his throat.

"He's good-looking," I whisper, "for a priest."

"Maybe he had a harelip or a hunchback that Saint Anne fixed." Colette hunches over and prepares for another imitation.

I pull Colette up by her shoulders. "Come on. Mom'll be inside in a minute. If you don't help, we'll be too late to meet Iza and the others." I pause. "And Maxim." Colette's got a huge crush on Maxim.

When Mom lets herself in, Colette is busy vacuuming around the cash register. I'm counting money.

"*Bonjour, mes filles*! Sorry I'm late. The buying trip took longer than we expected." Mom's face is flushed. "Thanks for watching the store, girls. You're my two angels."

Colette winks at me. Yeah, right, I think, you're some angel!

Now Colette is stuffing the vacuum cleaner back into the closet behind the counter. She doesn't wrap the electrical cord into a neat bundle the way she should, but I don't say anything. How many times have Mom and Dad told me that what Colette needs most is encouragement? And that we must love her exuberant personality. If you ask me, exuberant is code for annoying.

I hand Mom the cash from the register and the list of purchases made on credit and debit cards.

"Who's that priest you were talking to?" Colette asks Mom.

Mom unsnaps her purse and ignores Colette's question. "I'll see you two at home then. I'll set the alarm inside the store. You're on your bikes, aren't you? So you'll be leaving by the garage anyway. No fooling around, okay, Colette?"

Colette throws her arms up in the air. "Why do I always get blamed for fooling around, even when I haven't done anything?"

"Because you are always fooling around," I mutter under my breath.

Mom is by the front door, arming the alarm. She gives me a sharp look. "Look out for her. Remember, you're the big sister."

Aargh.

Most of the shops on Avenue Royale have garages and parking spots out back to make deliveries easier.

Even though our garage door is electric, it's ancient, and it makes a loud humming sound as it opens.

"Ready?" I ask Colette. The air is warm, and from where we are standing, we can see all the way down to Highway 138. Cars and trucks zip along in both directions. Somewhere in the distance, to the west of us, is the bridge to Île d'Orléans, and beyond that, about twenty miles away, is Quebec City.

Once I hit the switch, we'll have ninety seconds to get outside.

"Guillotine!" Colette calls out. Since we were little, Colette and I have made a game of running out while the garage door closes. She came up with the name Guillotine because if that door ever closed on us, it'd probably take off our heads. As we get bigger, the game's become harder. There is more of us that has to slip out before the door closes.

"Ready!" Colette says.

I hit the switch, and we take off.

I reach the end of the driveway first. I hear Colette panting behind me. She's running so hard I worry she'll crash into our bikes, which are chained together to a telephone pole. But Colette slides to a stop in front of the bikes. "That was fun," she says, "even if you beat me!"

Mom has already put out the recycling. My eyes land on a giant cardboard box with a picture of a two-foot-tall Jesus figurine on one side.

Then a really weird thing happens.

Jesus' eyes flash, as if he's alive and possibly angry at me.

For a second, I wonder if He is trying to send me a message. My shoulders stiffen.

Colette grabs my arm. "C'mon," she says, "let's go!"

When I look back at the box, Jesus' eyes are flat and dead.

Two

"Bless us, oh Lord, and these Thy gifts..." Mom bows her head as she prays.

I bow my head and say grace with Mom. I should be thinking about the Lord and His gifts, but Colette is distracting me. Again. She keeps tapping her fingers on the edge of the table. Even Dad is playing with his napkin.

Colette looks like Dad. She has his stocky build, dark laughing eyes and curly chestnut hair. I'm more like Mom. We're slim, with pale blue eyes, straight blond hair (although mine is thicker) and the same heart-shaped face. The women on Mom's side go gray early. Mom's only thirty-four, but her hair's already got gray streaks. I guess it'll happen to me too.

Mom's friend Lise—my friend Iza's mother—is always after Mom to dye her hair, but Mom won't. She's kind of an eco-freak. It started when Colette was four, after she was diagnosed with ADHD—Attention Deficit and Hyperactivity Disorder. Mom read online that eliminating household chemicals might help Colette. Of course, there's no way of knowing if it worked. All I know is the bottom of our bathtub's gray—a problem eco-cleanser won't fix—and Colette is still a royal pain.

Colette has one thing I wish I had. Boobs. Even though I'm sixteen, my chest is almost as flat as the dining-room table. Sometimes, when we're getting dressed in the upstairs bedroom we share, I sneak a peek at Colette's chest—her breasts are the size of grapefruits—and I feel a tug of jealousy. I know it isn't right, but I still do. What if I stay flat-chested forever?

Colette's moving her lips, but she isn't saying the words to the prayer out loud.

Dad is still playing with his napkin. Sometimes I wonder if he has a touch of ADHD too. When Mom looks up and catches Dad's eye, he stops.

Other than Dad's office behind the kitchen, the dining room is the only crucifix-free zone in our house. Dad freaked out a couple of weeks ago when Mom came home with another crucifix (a sample from a supplier) and tried to hang it on the wall across from the table. Her plan might have worked if she hadn't hung it right in Dad's line of vision.

"If there's one thing that spoils my appetite, Thérèse," Dad had said, shaking his head, "it's the sight of Jesus bleeding on the cross!" Then Dad closed his eyes, refusing to open them until Mom took down the crucifix.

The crucifix was made of resin, and Jesus was wearing a tan loincloth that looked like a diaper. "But this is such a lovely crucifix. See how lifelike our Savior's skin looks," Mom had said, stroking the resin as if it were flesh.

Dad banged his fist on the table. "My point exactly!"

"Calm down, Robert," Mom told him, patting his arm. "I'll find another place for it."

Dad shook his head again. "I'm sure you will."

When Dad gets upset, it's a lightning flash—over quickly and leaving the air feeling crisper afterward. "Let's kiss and make up," he'll say to Mom, puckering up his lips in a way that always makes Colette hoot.

"Not in front of the girls," Mom will say, blushing.

When Mom and Dad argue, it's usually about religion. She believes; he doesn't. They compromise when it comes to home décor. No crucifixes in Dad's office or the dining room. But there is a crucifix over the kitchen sink, one on either side of the blue velvet couch in the living room and one over every bed in our house. I wonder if Dad has to close his eyes when he and Mom have sex too. Not that I ever like to think about my parents having sex. What kid does?

Mom believes we need to be constantly reminded that Jesus sacrificed His life for us.

I'm not so sure that's necessary.

One thing Mom and Dad agree about, though, is raising us. They're both too strict, especially now that we're teenagers. I don't understand why they worry so much. I've never caused them any trouble and, except for her ADHD, Colette's not a bad kid either. Besides, it's hard to make trouble in a town this size, where everybody knows each other. Not to mention that we've got good Saint Anne watching out from every statue, key chain and nightlight.

Colette pops up from her chair when I ask her to help me clear the dishes. I know it's because she wants to see Maxim.

"Don't tell me you're going to McDonald's again," Mom says to us.

I know it's pathetic, but McDonald's is the coolest place in town to hang out. Other than the basilica (not exactly a hot spot for teens) and the other religious monuments, all we've got is the Sweet Heaven Candy Store and a couple of restaurants with names like L'Église and Pilgrims' Café.

I guess Mom wishes her two angels would spend less time at McDonald's and more time at home reading the Bible, the way she says she did when she was our age.

Mom runs Saintly Souvenirs, the souvenir shop she inherited after her parents died. Dad does the accounting—and the grocery shopping and cooking. He's always testing new recipes he finds online. Tonight we had braided asparagus spears with cranberry chicken over steamed rice.

"That's exactly where we're going." Colette answers for both of us. "Again."

Dad clears his throat. "We want the two of you home by ten thirty."

"Not a moment later," Mom adds, wiping her chin with her napkin.

"That's right," Dad says. The two of them exchange small smiles. Maybe it's because they disagree so much about religion that Mom and Dad seem extra-pleased when they agree about something.

Colette groans. "Ten thirty is so too early! Can't we—?"

"We'll be back on time," I say, catching Colette's eye and giving her a sharp look.

Colette mouths the words "Saint Ani" at me.

I glare at her, but she just smiles back at me.

It's almost completely dark when Colette and I leave. Our house is on a winding stretch of Avenue Royale, a quarter of a mile past the basilica and the souvenir shops. Because we're on the north side, the back of our house faces the rocky cliff that borders Ste-Anne-de-Beaupré on one side. From our bedroom window at the front of the house, we can look out at the basilica's green roof and silver spires and the 138.

There's only one street in town where you can't see the cliff behind you. That's Côte Ste-Anne, where Iza lives, past the farmhouse with the old stone well. When I was little, I used to like the feeling of living sandwiched between the cliff and the highway. It made me feel safe. But I'm starting to feel different. Sometimes this town makes me claustrophobic. Trapped in a too-small town with too-strict parents and a super-annoying little sister.

One day I'll be old enough to live on my own. I like imagining myself in Quebec City or Montreal, someplace where my neighbors won't know anything about me. Where I won't always have to look out for Colette. That's what I'm thinking when she taps my shoulder to offer me some of her new chocolate lip gloss.

That's the thing about Colette: just when you think you've had it with her, she does something sweet.

Colette's got a good heart. She really does. I need to try and be nicer to her. When Colette and I walk out to the street, we hear a sudden creaking, followed by the sound of someone's raspy breathing. It's coming from the upstairs balcony of the white clapboard house across the street, just a little down the hill from where we live. The house is small, but the balcony is as big as our living room.

Colette steps a little closer to me. "It's him," she says.

"Not so loud," I say. "He'll hear you."

"Why's he always spying on us?" At least now she's whispering.

"Maybe he just wants some fresh air. Besides, we used to spy on him."

"Yeah, but we were little. He's a grown man."

I take bigger steps to keep up with Colette. Though I would never admit it to her, I think Marco Leblanc is creepy too. In all the years we've lived across the street from him, he has never said more than "Good morning" or "Good afternoon" to us. Not even when we were little and Mom forced us to wish him a good day or ask him how he was whenever we passed him.

Eventually, even Mom gave up on trying to be friends with Marco. Which is unusual since Mom can make friends with a lamppost. Mom and Marco grew up together, but she says he pushed her away—that he pushed a lot of people away—over the years, and that even if it hurts, you've got to respect a person's feelings.

Marco owns the whole house. He inherited it from his parents. He lives upstairs—probably because the balcony is good for spying on his neighbors. The downstairs is rented out. He must have one of those electric stair lifts to get downstairs, but he sure doesn't use it much. Colette and I have never seen him leave his apartment. Not even once.

Marco gets his food delivered from the IGA, and once a week a nurse from the clinic comes to check on him. Once in a while he has other visitors. Mostly guys. I guess he hasn't gotten around to pushing them away yet.

We hear more creaking as Marco's wheelchair creeps along the edge of the balcony. I've heard how prisoners on death row pace in their cells. Marco "paces" back and forth in his wheelchair along the edge of his balcony. He paces all day and sometimes at night too.

He also lifts weights. In summer, most people here line their balconies with pots of geraniums; Marco lines his with free weights—dozens of chrome dumbbells that glimmer when the sun lands on them. Often, when we're biking to Saintly Souvenirs, Colette and I see Marco on his balcony. Then all at once, his head will disappear as he leans down to grab a weight in each hand and press it slowly to his chest.

Marco's lower body must be shriveled. I get grossed out if I even try to picture it. He got run over by a train when he was seventeen; Mom says it was because he had been drinking. But Marco's upper body looks like Arnold Schwarzenegger's, with muscles in places you didn't even know had muscles. In summer, Marco wears tight white undershirts that make the disproportion even creepier.

Marco has a rickety old wheelchair with thin worn tires—which explains the creaking. Because it's nearly dark, it's hard to make out the exact shape of the wheelchair, or of Marco sitting hunched in it. From where we are on the sidewalk, it's as if Marco is a giant bird of prey waiting for the right moment to pounce on us.

Mom says we shouldn't be afraid of Marco. "What harm can he do? The poor man has been confined to a wheelchair for nearly twenty years. We need to keep him in our prayers."

Dad says Marco is living proof there's no such thing as miracles. "If Saint Anne really was capable of miracles, wouldn't she have healed Marco—a man who has lived in her town all his life—by now?"

We're heading downhill, but the creaking and the raspy breathing sounds seem to be following us.

Colette grabs my arm.

I don't want to look back, but I feel this urge to make sure Marco's not following us—even though I know he can't be.

When I turn around, I can see, even in the dim light, that Marco has inched his wheelchair to the very edge of the balcony. His knees press against the railing.

When he speaks, his voice is even raspier than his breathing. The words come out like a bullfrog's croak.

"You two," he says, "are growing up."

And for a moment, I wish we weren't.

Three

Colette throws her shoulders back as we grab our milkshakes and head for our usual booth at McDonald's. I swear it's because she wants Maxim to notice her chest. Sometimes I can't believe we're related. If I was the one with grapefruit boobs, I'd never show them off like that.

Maxim is wearing a navy polo shirt with the collar popped up. He's sitting next to Iza and across from Josianne and Armand, but he looks up and smiles when he sees us coming. Maxim has powerful girl radar.

"Isn't he gorgeous?" Colette whispers.

"He's okay."

"Ex-cuse me. I forgot it's against your religion to notice boys."

"It's against my religion to be boy crazy. The way you are."

"How are my curls? Not too frizzy?"

"They're fine. Calm down, will you?"

"Being calm's no fun."

Josianne is practically sitting in Armand's lap. I still can't get used to the idea that those two are going out. Until last winter, we were all just a bunch of friends. Now Josianne and Armand are always looking for ways to get "private time." I know sexual feelings are normal, but I'm not quite ready to deal with them. And I wish my friends weren't either. Not to mention my little sister.

Iza is telling Maxim about her job at Cyclorama, this huge white and gold multi-sided building on the other side of Rue Regina. A lot of tourists see the giant *Cyclorama* sign from the highway and figure it's a humungous indoor bike track. Only when they get closer do they see the smaller letters that say *of Jerusalem*. Inside is a giant panoramic painting that tells the story of Jesus' life, complete with sound effects like lambs bleating and swords scraping.

"This guy was embarrassed to admit he made a mistake, so he bought a ticket," Iza is saying. "But I knew he'd rather be cycl—"

Colette doesn't let Iza finish her sentence. "Who *wouldn't* rather be cycling?" Colette says. I tug on her elbow, but she doesn't get the hint.

"Hey, An-ette!" (Anette is Iza's nickname for us— a combination of our two names.) Iza moves closer to Maxim to make room for one of us. I grab the spot, though it means I'm going to have to watch Armand and Josianne groping each other all night.

"So I heard you're gonna be in Ste-Anne-de-Beaupré all summer," Colette says to Maxim. "That's so amazing. Wow. All summer. Like I said, that's really great." The girl doesn't breathe when she talks.

Maxim doesn't seem to mind Colette's exuberance. When he smiles, I notice his teeth are very white; one of the front ones is chipped. Though I'd never tell Colette, I think Maxim is kind of hot, in a boy-band sort of way.

"Do you use tooth whitener?" Colette asks him.

Maxim laughs, then looks down at the table, which makes me think he probably does.

Iza nudges Maxim. "That's Colette. She's special." Iza must notice my back stiffen when she says that. "What I mean is…Colette's the kind of person who says what she thinks. It's refreshing, really. Like the time she asked our French teacher, Monsieur Leduc, why he smelled of beer at eight fifteen in the morning."

Maxim slaps the table and laughs. "What'd he say?"

"He said he used beer for shampoo. Only, I told him it smelled more like he used beer for mouthwash." Colette laughs so hard at the memory she snorts chocolate milkshake out her nose.

Everyone else laughs too, and my back relaxes. It's okay if I think Colette is a pain—I'm her sister. But I don't like other kids, even Iza, saying anything bad about her.

"Move over, lovebirds," Colette tells Josianne and Armand, and they make room for her on their side of the booth.

"So you guys are working at the basilica parking lot, right?" I say to Armand and Maxim.

"Yup. It's a great gig," Armand says.

Josianne gives Armand a dreamy look, as if working in a parking lot is as exciting as being a rock star.

"How's it going anyway—staying with your grand-mother?" Armand asks Maxim.

Colette is bouncing in the booth. It's a small bounce that's coming from her hips, but it'll get bigger. It always does. "Who's your grandmother?"

"Hélène Dupuis. I bet in a town this size, you know her, right?"

Colette's not only bouncing now, she's reaching across the table for Maxim's hand. What's she thinking?

Of course I know the answer. She isn't thinking. Colette is a very impulsive person. If I liked a guy, I'd never grab at him like that. I'd be more subtle. Or I'd wait for him to take my hand.

"Tante Hélène's your grandmother?" Colette asks.

I kick her under the table.

"Why'd you kick me?" she says.

Now I want to kill her. "It was an accident," I say, glaring. But at least she's stopped grabbing for Maxim's hand. Besides, I'm sure she was about to blurt out how we all call Maxim's grandmother Crazy Tante Hélène.

Crazy Tante Hélène calls herself an herbalist. She has long white hair and she lives down by the 138 in a rundown house with a lawn that looks like it's never been mowed. Everyone else in town hates dandelions— but not Crazy Tante Hélène. Her front yard looks like a dandelion farm. She prescribes dandelion tea for people with nervous conditions. I know, because Mom bought some for Colette after the ADHD medication she was taking gave her insomnia and made her stop eating.

"Staying with my gramma's okay. Only this morning, when I told her I had a sore throat, she made me drink tea with garlic." Maxim gags at the memory.

Colette giggles. "I've heard of Earl Grey, I've heard of Sleepytime, but garlic tea? No way! That is so gross!"

"Did it help?" Iza asks.

"Now that you mention it—my throat feels fine."

Colette leans across the table, chest-first. "Here, lemme see if you smell like garlic. No, you smell really good." Her cheeks are flushed. So are mine—just from watching Colette. I don't understand how she can be so bold. Colette doesn't have a shy bone in her body. When it comes to boys, all two hundred and six of my bones are shy. "Hey, wanna see my imitations of the pilgrims who come to our shop?" she asks Maxim.

"Sure." Maxim is eyeing Colette the way a bee eyes a freshly opened flower, circling before he makes a landing, and there isn't anything I can do to stop it.

"Colette's really good at imitations," Armand says.

"Yeah, really good," Josianne adds.

Iza taps my leg under the table. We both hate the way Josianne agrees with whatever Armand says. She never used to be like that.

I think about giving Colette another kick, but I know she'll say something if I do. I just hope she won't go too far with those imitations. What if she starts groping imaginary penises again? My ears heat up just thinking about it.

A McDonald's employee—a middle-aged woman wearing a hairnet—is collecting trash. "You kids done with those trays?" she asks. The pin on her blouse says *Evelyne*.

"Yes, we are, Evelyne." Maxim looks right at her when he hands her our trays. "That's a nice name. And hey, thanks a lot."

Evelyne blushes.

It's Colette's idea to walk Maxim to his grandmother's when we leave McDonald's. There's a rusty watering can on Tante Hélène's front porch. Her kitchen light is on. Maybe she's making dandelion tea. I hope her kettle's in better shape than her watering can.

"I hope I'll see you again soon," Maxim says when we leave him at the porch.

"Who do you mean?" Colette asks. "Me? Or her?"

I don't know whether to laugh or feel embarrassed.

"I mean both of you, of course." Then Maxim turns to Colette, and I catch him peeking at her cleavage. Even in the dark, I can see that Colette's whole face is glowing. "I'm guessing you don't go to church on Sundays."

"Of course I do," Colette says.

Now I really want to laugh. Colette hasn't gone to church since Mom forced her to at Easter.

Four

D ad whistles. "My, you girls look pretty!"
The three of us are leaving for church. Mom's
wearing her best dress; it's white with black polka dots
and tight at the waist. Colette and I are wearing pleated
skirts. Mine is sky blue; hers, which she's hiked way up
over her knees, is the color of red wine. I've got on my
white blouse with the frilly collar; Colette's wearing a
low-cut pale pink tank top.

There's a *No T-shirts* sign inside the basilica, but I've
never seen anyone get kicked out for wearing a T-shirt
or tank top. I guess these days churches need all the
customers they can get.

I caught Mom eyeing Colette's tank top and short skirt when we came downstairs, but she must've decided not to say anything. She's probably just happy Colette is feeling religious. I don't want to burst Mom's bubble and tell her Colette's more interested in Maxim than in Jesus.

"You girls look so pretty," Dad says again, "I'm tempted to come along."

"Do you mean it?" Mom asks, watching Dad's face. Even after so many years together, I think Mom still hopes Dad'll suddenly see the light.

Dad is right though. Mom looks prettier than usual. She's piled her hair on top of her head and is even wearing eye shadow (made from all natural ingredients, of course).

Dad strokes Mom's cheek. "Not really," he says. I saw him glancing at the newspaper before, and I bet he's looking forward to plopping down on the couch with the paper and our cat, Eeyore. They are, as Dad's always saying, the only two guys in a house full of women.

"Have a good time, Thérèse. Enjoy the company of both your angels." Dad gives Mom a peck on the lips, pulls on one of Colette's curls and tweaks my nose. It's how he always says goodbye to us.

"We'll tell the Lord and good Saint Anne hi from you," I tell him.

Dad laughs. "Those two are too busy to bother with an old sinner like me."

Marco Leblanc is already outside, lifting weights on his balcony. We hear him groan as he presses the weights to his chest. Mom waves when we pass him, but he doesn't bother waving back.

Because the sidewalk is so narrow and there isn't much traffic this far along Avenue Royale, the three of us walk side-by-side on the street. Mom loops one arm through mine, the other through Colette's. "I'm so glad, Colette, that you're coming to Mass," Mom says. "This feels like a fresh beginning."

Mom doesn't notice Colette wink at me. "My girls"—now Mom is speaking more to herself than to us—"are growing up."

I can't help shivering. That's exactly what Marco said the other night.

సా

It takes twenty minutes to walk to the basilica. It's quicker when we aren't wearing high heels. On the way, we talk about the store (it's nearly time to change the window display), the weather (not a cloud in the sky), and our plans to have a picnic supper at the canyon (if the weather stays good).

In the distance, the traffic is building on the 138 near the exit that leads into town. Impatient drivers honk their horns. A crow flies overhead. I wonder what he thinks of all the traffic.

All year long, Catholics from all over northeastern Quebec come to Sunday Mass in Ste-Anne-de-Beaupré. We have the most beautiful church in the province and also one of the oldest. It dates all the way back to the seventeenth century.

We stop chatting once we pass the last of the souvenir shops. On Sundays, everyone in about a block and a half radius of the church is quiet before Mass. It's an unofficial rule. I guess the idea is to clear our minds so we can think about God.

Just when I am trying to do that, Colette nudges me. "I don't see him. Do you see him?" she whispers. I shrug and pretend not to understand who she's talking about.

Closer to the basilica grounds, I notice a little girl walking between her parents. She is wearing a gauzy pink dress, a straw hat with a pink bow, and white gloves. That's how Mom dressed us for church when we were little. I wonder if in ten years the little girl will be wearing a skimpy tank top like Colette's, or if she'll be a more modest dresser like me.

We're about to pass the water fountain with the bronze statue of Saint Anne and baby Mary in the middle. Water shoots up from openings in the ground and more water drips down from the giant basin that holds Saint Anne and Mary. On hot summer Sundays when we were little, Colette always wanted to take off her gloves and good shoes and run through the water. Of course, even then I knew we couldn't.

Colette pulls me closer to the fountain. She closes her eyes and grins as the mist sprays her face. I pull away. I don't want to get wet.

Once we're past the fountain, Colette stands on her tiptoes to peer over the railroad tracks into the parking lot. She's forgotten the *No talking* rule. "There's Armand, and, oh, there's—" She's waving like mad now.

"Stop it," I tell her.

A woman walking in the other direction wags her finger at me.

Colette covers her mouth so she won't laugh.

We follow Mom into the basilica. There's traffic here too, especially by the wheelchair ramp. Because I know it's important to be kind to disabled people, I smile at a woman waiting by the ramp. She's in a wheelchair, with a plaid blanket over her legs. I try to concentrate on her face, not her withered legs.

There are three arched entrances, and we pass through the center one, which is the biggest. Mom and I stop to dip our fingers in the holy water in one of the granite fonts at the back of the basilica, then make the sign of the cross over our hearts. Colette does the same; Mom pats her elbow.

Colette says what she hates most about church is the rules. How we have to dip our fingers in the font, genuflect when we pass the tabernacle, walk down the center aisle before we receive Communion and use a side aisle when we return to our pews.

I like the rules. It's not the sort of thing I can explain to Colette, but with so much changing around me all the time—the way my friends have suddenly gotten interested in sex, my feelings about life in this town—there's something comforting about rules. As if there's a solid place to rest in the middle of the chaos that comes from all the changes.

I take a deep breath as I walk into the oratory. Though Mom and I come here every Sunday, its beauty also takes me a little by surprise. The vaulted ceiling seems to go up and up forever like a golden sky. I even love the smell—musty and sweet at the same time.

We take our seats in the fifth row. In the pews in front of us are clergymen, the mayor and his wife, the city councilors and their families. We always sit in the fifth row. When Mom's parents were alive, they sat here too. I guess it's a little like always sitting in the same booth at McDonald's.

The Dandurands, who own the L'Église restaurant, are in our row too. Monsieur Dandurand nods when he sees us. I think it bugs him that Dad isn't here. I don't know if it's because Monsieur Dandurand disapproves of nonbelievers, or because he wishes his wife would let him stay home and read the paper on Sunday morning too.

Colette makes a tunnel with one hand and brings it to her eye. I know what she's doing: looking at the stained glass windows and pretending her hand is a kaleidoscope. It's another thing we did when we were little. We'd look, then blink, then look again. The yellows, oranges, blues and greens would come together, then separate, then come together again. The parts were most beautiful when they made a whole. "C'mon," Colette whispers. "Do it."

"I'm too old for games," I whisper back.

Someone coughs and then clears his throat, a baby cries at the back of the basilica and his mother shushes him. Otherwise, the basilica is quiet.

Madame Dandurand pokes her husband with her purse and tips her head toward a priest who is about to sit down in the front row. Mom is watching him too. It's the handsome dark-haired priest—the one Mom was talking to last week. Madame Dandurand whispers, "I didn't know he was back from Africa," to her husband.

Even the baby stops crying when the choir begins to sing in the balcony and Father Lanctot and the altar boys proceed from the back of the oratory down the center aisle to the altar. The altar boys go first. They're dressed in white satin robes. The one in the middle carries a golden cross with a crucified Jesus on it. The other two are carrying tall wooden candlesticks. They press the candlesticks to their chests and walk slowly so the flames won't go out.

I hear the swish of Father Lanctot's black cassock. "Where's his Kleenex?" Colette whispers. My eyes move to Father Lanctot's sleeve and sure enough, like always, a piece of balled up Kleenex is poking out. Father Lanctot has a permanently runny nose and a gross habit of reusing his old Kleenex.

Mom's got the look on her face she always gets at church—as if she has been transported someplace wonderful. She hasn't noticed Colette whispering. I'd like to go someplace wonderful too. Only it's hard with

Colette shifting in her seat next to me and whispering about Kleenex.

Father Lanctot genuflects before the altar. His eyes are watery and his face is as lined as a map. "It's lucky he only has to go down on one knee," Colette whispers. "If he used both knees, he might not be able to get back up."

I don't want to giggle. But there's something about being in a place where I'm not supposed to giggle that makes me more prone to giggling. And Colette knows it. Monsieur Dandurand gives us a steely look.

I force myself to concentrate on Father Lanctot's face. He has turned toward us. "May the Lord be with you."

"And also with you," the congregation responds. Everyone is watching Father Lanctot—except Colette. She's looking to the right. I turn a little too, to see what's distracting her. I should have guessed: Maxim is standing inside the arched doorway, his orange security vest slung over his arm.

When I look back at Colette, she's got the same look on her face as Mom.

❧

As soon as it's time for Communion, Colette needs to pee. At least that's what she tells Mom.

Communion is my favorite part of Mass. I love the feeling I get when the Host—the thin round wafer Catholics believe is miraculously transformed into the body of Christ—is melting on my tongue. That's when I'm most sure the Lord's spirit is alive in me and in all living creatures. Even Colette.

The dark-haired priest is at the altar now, holding a gold chalice with extra wafers. When it's Mom's turn to receive Communion, I watch him, but he shows no sign of recognizing her. It's as if he's making a point of looking over her head and out at the congregation.

Father Lanctot hands Mom the Host, and she puts it on her tongue. In the old days, you'd open your mouth and the priest would pop the Host right in. That was before people worried so much about germs and disease.

When it's my turn, I feel the handsome priest's eyes on me. On my face, my hair and especially on my eyes. I get this weird feeling he's looking inside me. He smiles, and when he does, his face softens and he looks even more handsome. I can't decide if I should smile back. Can he see I'm blushing?

Then, just like that, the moment is over and I'm following Mom back to our pew. My hands and feet feel tingly. I was so busy thinking about the handsome priest

I forgot to think about our Savior. The Host has melted on my tongue without my even noticing it. All that's left is a papery taste.

ॐ

"You shouldn't have taken off like that," I say, wagging my finger at Colette after we file out of the basilica. "You missed Communion. And I bet you didn't even have to pee. I bet you were busy flirting."

Colette puts her hands on her hips. "Can I ask you something? Why are you always trying to ruin my fun?"

"Who says Sunday Mass is supposed to be fun?"

Of course, Colette has an answer to that. "If it was fun, more people would come."

I take a deep breath. "It's just not right to miss Communion," I tell her.

"I'm not like you. I'm not obsessed with what's right. Besides, the last thing I want—the very last thing—is to take a stale wafer from some decrepit old priest." Colette has started to rock from one foot to the other.

"And would you quit doing that?" I tell her. "You're making me dizzy."

"Quit what?"

"The rocking!" I try not to shout, but my voice comes out louder than I want it to. People are turning to look at us.

Colette is still rocking, like a swing that keeps going even when no one's on it. "I can't help it," she says in a small voice that only makes me feel angrier with her.

Five

Maybe I was too hard on Colette. I shouldn't have bawled her out in public. She can't help the rocking. It's a symptom of her ADHD. So I decide to make it up to her by asking Mom if it's okay to invite Maxim and his grandmother to our picnic.

"It's a lovely idea," Mom says. "I've always liked Tante Hélène. It isn't right that people in town call her crazy. She's just a free spirit."

Mom's taking her own car to the canyon. She wants to stop in first at Saintly Souvenirs to check on Clara Bergeron, who works in the shop on Sundays. "You know how nervous Clara gets. I'll just pop by and make sure things are under control."

When Colette hears that Maxim and his grand-mother are coming and that it was all my idea, she is too excited to accuse me of acting saintly. She rushes upstairs, disappearing into her side of our closet. The hangers start clattering, and soon there's a mountain of clothes on her bed. "Too warm. Too fancy for a hike," she says, tossing more clothes onto the pile. Finally she settles on a pair of khaki short-shorts and a tank top with a skull and crossbones on it.

When Colette puts on her matching skull and cross-bones earrings, I decide to put on my earrings with the gold crosses. One of us has to look respectable.

The Ste-Anne Canyon is east of town on the 138. We take Dad's van, stopping to get Maxim and his grand-mother. Iza is coming too, but she's taking the Mini Cooper she got when she turned sixteen. Iza's dad is the richest person in Ste-Anne-de-Beaupré. He owns most of the buildings on Avenue Royale, and his company is also behind a new condo complex on the edge of the cliff.

"Will you ask Iza if she'll give Maxim and me a ride home in the convertible? Please!" Colette asked, jumping up and down next to me while I was on the phone with Iza. And because I wanted to make things up to Colette, I asked Iza, who said yes. Colette was so excited, she danced around our room.

Tante Hélène is watering her dandelions when we drive up. She's wearing a floppy faded sunhat and a flowery apron over denim overalls. She does look kind of crazy.

I offer her my spot in front, next to Dad, but Tante Hélène refuses it. "Don't go treating me like an old woman! I'm only seventy-five," she says as she hops up into the backseat.

Maxim's got a jug of lemonade. "Gramma's special recipe," he says.

"I added some mint from my herb garden," Tante Hélène explains. I must say that for someone her age, Tante Hélène's in pretty good shape. Maybe it's all those herbs. "The combination of lemon and mint has a wonderful purifying effect on the digestive system," she says.

"And thank god there's no garlic in it," Maxim says, winking at Colette and me.

Tante Hélène ruffles Maxim's hair. "You've got your grandfather's sense of humor. He used to tease me too, though he never complained about my throat tonic."

Colette is sitting next to Maxim, who is balancing the lemonade between his feet. She rattles off all the food Mom's packed in the picnic basket. "Tuna salad and egg salad sandwiches on whole wheat. Which do you like better, Maxim—tuna or egg? Most people like tuna better.

Mom also made sandwiches with cream cheese and Dad's crabapple jelly. Then there's Dad's homemade cole-slaw, potato salad from the IGA, fruit salad—but there aren't any mangoes in it, in case you like mangoes. Ani's allergic. She once ate some mango ice cream and her lips got swollen. Then her throat started to close up. She was choking and everything! There's another dessert too, but I'm not saying what. And don't you try to make me!"

Colette moves in so close to Maxim their thighs are touching. I think she likes being pressed up against him. I can't imagine behaving that way or feeling so free.

"C'mon, tell me," Maxim says.

Colette doesn't even pretend to put up a fight. "Okay then, I'll tell you. Dad made strawberry bars—with strawberries from Île d'Orléans. They taste like heaven."

"Are you giving away family secrets again?" Dad asks from behind the wheel.

Iza is waiting in the parking lot when we get there, and Mom drives up five minutes later. There are a lot of tourists here today, judging from the license plates. In the ticket line, we hear people speaking Dutch and Italian and Spanish.

"*¿Cómo estás?*" Maxim asks a pretty girl with thick black hair and turquoise sneakers. She has the smallest waist I've ever seen.

"*¿Hablas español?*" she asks, smiling, but it turns out *¿Cómo estás?* is all Maxim can say in Spanish. Still, using sign language, Maxim offers to take a photo of the girl and her family using their camera. They want to pose by the giant plastic woodpecker near the front entrance.

"His grandfather was a ladies' man too," Tante Hélène says as Maxim snaps the photo. She makes it sound like a compliment.

Colette tugs on Maxim's sleeve before he can ask for the Spanish girl's email address. "C'mon," she says. "Let's go see the falls!"

The woods are dense, and we have to hike to reach the waterfall.

"Doesn't the air smell divine?" Tante Hélène sniffs at the air as if she wants to eat it.

Mom turns her face up to the sky, closes her eyes and smiles. She has the same look on her face she gets at Sunday Mass.

Maxim makes a show of taking his grandmother's arm. Tante Hélène giggles as if she's in high school too. Colette is on her other side, asking her all about herbal cures.

"You see those birch trees?" Tante Hélène says. "Birch bark tea is excellent for treating arthritis. And you can make a paste with it that helps fight warts."

At this rate, it's going to take forever to get to our picnic spot. Especially if Tante Hélène keeps stopping to inspect flora ("What a splendid patch of coltsfoot!") and fauna ("Did you see that remarkable ladybug? She's orange, not red. Quite unusual in these parts, really.").

The canyon has three suspended bridges, and we have to cross the highest one to see the falls. Already I can feel the dewy spray from the waterfall on my face.

The cable bridge lists a little to one side when we cross it. One hundred and eighty feet below us, the Ste-Anne-du-Nord River plunges into a rocky gorge. Looking down makes me queasy, so I focus on the thick woods at the other side.

And there's the waterfall!

"It's higher than Niagara Falls!" Colette tells Maxim. Because she's bouncing again, Colette makes the whole bridge sway.

"Colette!" Dad says sternly. "You're going to make the rest of us seasick!"

Colette stops bouncing, but the bridge keeps swaying.

Once we make it over the bridge, we leave the path. Dad leads us to a spot where the ground is flat, and spreads out our checkered tablecloth. Iza helps Mom and me unpack sandwiches. Maxim fills reusable plastic cups

(Mom won't buy any other kind) with lemonade. Tante Hélène keeps offering to help, but Mom and Dad won't let her. "My goodness," Tante Hélène says, looking down at her lap, "why didn't someone tell me I was still wearing my apron?"

Dad laughs. "We thought it was part of your outfit."

"No wonder people call me crazy!"

Colette has disappeared—she has a habit of disappearing whenever there's work to do—but now she's back, with a handful of birch bark she's peeled off a yellow birch tree.

"That's very kind, my dear," Tante Hélène says when Colette gives her the birch bark. "I just hope you didn't peel off too much and scar the tree."

"Oh no." Colette covers her mouth with her hand.

"I'm sure the tree is fine," Tante Hélène tells her, "but it's good to know. For the next time. Now will you pass me some of that lovely coleslaw?"

Maxim hands Iza and me each a cup of lemonade.

Tante Hélène has stretched out and is resting on her elbows. She sure doesn't act like an old lady. And with the sun shining on her face, you can hardly see the wrinkles. "Ahh," she says, looking up at the falls, "this is what I call a miracle."

Mom looks at the falls and the forest and our picnic lunch. "It's the Lord's work," she says. "All of it."

Dad takes a bite of his tuna sandwich.

In science class we learned that the canyon and the falls were created by Precambrian rock, the river and millions of years of erosion. But I know what Mom would say to that: "Who do you think created Precambrian rock, the river and erosion?" It's hard to argue with someone who's religious.

Tante Hélène sighs. "Whoever's work it is, it's still a miracle."

Dad groans when Mom's cell phone buzzes and she fishes it out of her backpack. Though we've got a family cell-phone plan, Dad refuses to get a phone. "I suppose you think cell phones are the Lord's work too," he mutters under his breath.

"Hello," Mom says into the phone.

I can hear loud ringing and Clara's voice at the other end of the line. "It's the alarm!" Clara is shouting. "I can't turn it off for the life of me! I've tried everything!"

Mom brushes some leaves off her hiking pants. "Don't panic, Clara. The alarm's programmed to go off by itself." Mom's speaking loudly so Clara will hear her over the noise. "The alarm company should phone in

47

a few minutes. Just explain what's happened. Give them the password. Everything will be fine. I promise."

I can't hear what Clara is saying now, but Mom is nodding sympathetically. "Try taking some deep breaths," Mom suggests. Her forehead crinkles up the way it does when she's worried. "You don't sound good, Clara. We're at the canyon, but I can be there in about half an hour."

Dad reaches for the phone. "Let me try to help her." Then he lowers his voice so Clara won't hear him, "This is ridiculous, Thérèse. There's no reason for you to go all the way back. It's just a damned alarm."

Mom flinches. She hates when Dad swears.

"It's no use, Robert," Mom says, waving him off. "You know how nervous Clara gets. I'm afraid she's having a full-fledged panic attack. She says her heart is racing. What if she goes rushing out of the store and leaves the cash unattended?"

"Okay then, I'll drive," Dad says.

Mom squeezes his hand. "No, no. I'll manage. Besides, I'm in my own car. You've been trapped inside all week like a mole working on the accounts; you need the fresh air more than any of us. Besides, *chéri*"—she pats Dad's belly—"unless you stop eating strawberry bars, you'll never be able to keep up with me on the hiking trail."

"Why don't I go?" Maxim offers. "I can look at the alarm. I'm good at fixing things, aren't I, Gramma?"

"You certainly are. That boy worked miracles with my blender when he arrived two weeks ago. His grandfather was handy too."

Colette pops up from her spot. "Well then, I'm coming too!"

Why am I not surprised?

ॐ

Things get way quieter after Colette leaves. But the mood is also a little...well...flat. We can always count on Colette to keep a party—or a picnic—going. Tante Hélène has noticed a patch of dry skin on Dad's elbow. She says chamomile can relieve the itching. Dad forgets to cover his mouth when he yawns. He's about as interested in herbal remedies as he is in Jesus.

Iza has another Cyclorama story. "The sound system got stuck and those sheep were bleating nonstop for twenty minutes. Honestly, I wanted to shoot myself. Some people wanted their money back."

Tante Hélène eats two sandwiches and asks for more coleslaw.

About an hour later, when my cell phone starts to vibrate, Dad groans. "This new generation," he tells Tante Hélène, "they can't go for a picnic without a cell phone."

I answer. It's Colette and it's hard to make out what she's saying because she's making weird gulping noises. "Come right away...Tell...tell Dad there's been a terrible... accident. It's Mom."

My mouth won't work. I want to know more, but I can't form the questions. Even if I could, it wouldn't help. Colette has hung up. The last thing I hear is the sound of her gulping and from somewhere in the distance, the piercing screech of an ambulance siren.

Six

I feel as if I'm under water. I can hear voices, but they sound gurgly, like they're coming through bubbles. "Don't worry about me," Tante Hélène is saying. Then there's more gurgling. "Iza will drive me back, won't you, dear?"

"Just go!" Iza's hand is on the small of my back, pushing me forward. Her fingers are warm, but my back is very, very cold.

"Godspeed!" Tante Hélène calls out after us.

We're moving so fast I don't even feel the spray from the waterfall on my face as we pass. But I hear twigs crunching under my feet and the sound of Dad panting. He might not be in as good shape as Mom, but right now, he's flying down the trail in front of me. I spot the back of his baseball cap before it disappears behind an aspen tree.

"Did Colette say anything else? Anything?" Dad's voice echoes in the forest. I'm surprised by how normal he sounds.

I'm finally able to get some words out. "Only that there was an accident," I say. "And that we should come right away." I feel my legs shaking underneath me. I don't mention the ambulance. I'm afraid if I do I'll cry.

"Emergency. Sorry. Emergency," Dad says as we elbow past happy picnickers headed in the opposite direction. An hour ago, we were happy too. Dad's T-shirt and cap are drenched in sweat. The brush is scratching my arms and legs, but I don't care. We have to get to Mom.

I try telling myself Colette was exaggerating—the way she does when she's doing imitations. But then why the ambulance? Maybe it was just background noise. But the siren sounded loud—and close.

If only the accident turns out to be nothing—or at least nothing too serious. Like a broken arm or leg. That'd be bad, but not the end of the world. Why did Colette use the word *terrible*? She could have said *bad*, but she said *terrible*. Terrible is worse than bad. Way worse.

There isn't time to get down on my knees and pray, but inside my head I'm praying like crazy. Please, God, protect Mom. Don't let her die. Please. I'll do anything you want me to—if only Mom's okay.

Dad turns around to check that I'm still behind him. He nods and gives me a tight smile. I'm panting now too.

"Dad," I say in a small voice when we're finally in the van and heading down the steep stretch of highway that leads from the canyon into the town of Beaupré, one town east of ours. "I didn't tell you, but when Colette phoned, I heard an ambulance."

Dad sucks in his breath. "Dear God," he whispers. In all my life, I don't think I've ever heard Dad use the word *God* before.

There's a thick crowd of people where we park the car behind Saintly Souvenirs. "What in God's name happened?" Dad shouts as we push our way through.

That's twice, I think. My world is now officially upside down.

I see Monsieur and Madame Dandurand and Maxim. Their faces look very serious. Clara's there too, the skin around her eyes looking pink and puffy. A group of tourists is standing beside a nearby car. They're putting on sunscreen, but I can sense their curiosity.

"Why don't you give me your keys, Robert?" Monsieur Dandurand says to Dad. "It's better if I drive you and Ani to Quebec City—to the hospital. Colette went in the ambulance. With Thérèse." His voice drops when he says Mom's name.

Dad's face has turned to stone. Gray stone. He hands Monsieur Dandurand the keys.

If we're going to the hospital, then Mom isn't dead. If she was dead, someone would have told us, right?

Clara grabs Dad's arm. "I'm so sorry," she says, gulping back tears. At first, Dad can hardly look at her.

The doors to the van click when Monsieur Dandurand unlocks them.

Clara won't let go of Dad's arm. "What happened, Clara?" Dad is asking her. "Why isn't anyone telling me anything?"

Clara is still clutching Dad's arm. "She told me to go home and relax—that she was closing up early. She wanted to surprise you and get back to your pic—" Clara's voice breaks. She swallows and starts again. "I stopped at L'Église for ice tea. That's when we heard the ambulance. It was the garage door...She got caught under it."

Clara releases Dad's arm.

"Shit," Dad says, punching the van door. "Shit, shit, shit."

Monsieur Dandurand winces. I can't tell if it's because of Mom's accident or Dad's swearing.

I tug on Dad's sleeve. "We have to go."

Dad lets me buckle his seatbelt. He looks out the window, but I get the feeling he's not seeing anything. Is he as scared as I am?

Monsieur Dandurand doesn't wait for the light on Avenue Royale to turn green. When we reach the on-ramp for the 138, he checks for oncoming cars—and guns it. I bet he doesn't usually drive like this. From my spot in the backseat, I can see fat round beads of sweat on Dad's cheeks and nose and over his lips. "Did you see her?" he asks Monsieur Dandurand. "Could she speak?"

Every muscle in my body tenses as I wait for Monsieur Dandurand's answer. Even my toes feel tense.

Monsieur Dandurand doesn't lift his eyes from the road. He's talking to the windshield. "I ran over when we heard the siren. She could speak," he says, and now I notice he is tightening his grip on the steering wheel. There are wispy black hairs on his knuckles. "But she couldn't move her legs."

After that, none of us says anything. We whiz by other cars and trucks. All I see are flashes of color—green grass, blue sky, green road signs with white lettering—and about twenty minutes later, the narrow gray streets of old Quebec City.

Monsieur Dandurand pulls up in front of the emergency room at L'Hôtel-Dieu Hospital. "I'll meet you two inside and bring you the keys," he tells Dad. "Constance said she'd pick me up."

Dad takes hold of Monsieur Dandurand's elbow. Saintly Souvenirs and L'Église are next door to each other, but before today, I doubt whether Dad and Monsieur Dandurand have ever discussed anything except the weather or how business is in town. "Thanks," Dad tells him. "Thanks for everything."

"We'll pray for her," Monsieur Dandurand says in a quiet voice.

"Thanks for that too."

Everything about the emergency-room waiting area is beige—the walls, chairs, even the doors. It's packed with people. One man's arm is in a makeshift sling; a woman holds an icepack over her cheek; someone else—I can't tell if it's a man or a woman—is snoring. Some people are reading newspapers and books. A kid is sitting on the floor, building a block castle.

Just as Dad and I are about to line up at the registration desk, a set of steel doors swings open and Colette runs out. Her dark eyes have a wild look.

"Daddy!" she wails, and everyone in the waiting room turns around—even the kid building the castle and the person who was asleep. Dad catches Colette in his arms like she's a football. She's weeping harder than she did when she was little and kids at school teased her for bouncing too much or calling out when it wasn't her turn.

"How is she?" Dad asks, wiping the tears from Colette's face with the back of his hand.

"Is she paralyzed?" I ask.

Colette's voice comes out muffled. "The doctors are examining her now. They told me to wait out here. They told me to tell you to wait too."

Dad lets go of Colette. "To hell with that!" he shouts, and now people are looking at him like he's some crazy person who needs to be restrained. "Ani," he says, grabbing my shoulder, "look after your sister. I'm going in there! Now!"

Seven

I take a deep breath and straighten my shoulders. It's up to me to be the strong one. Dad's gone berserk; Colette is crumpled in the seat next to me, looking like one of our old stuffed dolls after Eeyore tried to eat her. And Mom—I'm afraid to think about what shape Mom's in.

A nurse from the registration desk goes storming into the ER after Dad. "Sir, excuse me, Sir, but I'm afraid you have to follow the rules like everybody else."

We can hear Dad's voice through the steel doors. "To hell with rules! I need to see my wife!"

The nurse comes back out, looking flushed and shaking her head, but Dad's still in there.

Colette isn't saying a word. And she's not moving either—not tapping her feet or her hands, not wriggling in her seat.

"Should I get you some water?"

No answer. I get the water because I don't know what else to do for her. I bring the water in one of those disposable cups they use for mouthwash at the dentist's. I can just imagine Mom debating the pros and cons of paper cups. Please, God, let her be all right.

Colette sips the water. She's acting so out of it, you'd think she'd had the accident, not Mom. But I don't say so. I promised Dad I'd look after her. Still, that doesn't mean I can't ask questions. And I can't wait any longer.

I squeeze her elbow. "Tell me what happened." I make sure to keep my voice gentle. Colette can't be pushed.

She shakes her head.

A lady with frizzy blond hair sitting across from us puts down the book she's reading. I can tell it's some trashy romance novel because there's a half-naked woman on the cover drooling over a half-naked guy carrying a sword. The lady could at least try to pretend she's not eavesdropping. Why can't people mind their own business? And what makes other people's troubles so interesting anyhow?

I run my fingers through Colette's curls the way I used to when we were little. Her hair is just as soft as it was then. "C'mon, Colette." I whisper so the snoopy lady won't hear.

Colette is staring at her feet. "Maxim fixed the alarm. There was something wrong with the sensor. Clara was such a mess, Mom told her to go right home. Then Mom got the idea we should go back to the falls and surprise you guys. She told me and Maxim to go out and wait by car—that she'd close up and meet us out back. Maxim said we should help her close up. I told him no."

Colette hasn't taken her eyes off her feet. Now she's starting to rock in her seat. She rocks when she's really upset. Mom says Colette even did it in her crib some-times. Something about the rocking motion comforts her.

I pat Colette's arm. "Then what happened?"

"I didn't want to help Mom close." I can barely hear her. "I wanted to be alone with Maxim." Colette is rocking faster, leaning all the way into the back of the seat, then dropping her head as she moves forward. Watching her is making me dizzy.

"We were out on the street. I heard Mom calling, but I pretended not to hear. Then she called again, and Maxim said we had to go back. I didn't see her at first. I thought she'd be standing up." Colette is crying now. "But I heard her. She was whimpering, Ani. And then

I saw her—under the garage door. Her eyes were open. You know what she said?"

I'm digging my fingernails into the plastic armrests. I don't want to picture Mom pinned under the garage door, but the image is already taking shape in my mind.

"She said, 'Thank God. I thought you were going to leave me here.'"

I put my arms around Colette and hold her until she finally stops rocking. I think she needed to tell someone.

The woman with the frizzy hair sighs and picks up her book.

"Dad?" I say when I feel a warm hand on my shoulder. But it's Monsieur Dandurand with Dad's keys. "You should get back to L'Église," I tell him. "We're so grateful for everything you've done." But when Monsieur Dandurand insists on waiting till Dad comes out of the ER with some news, I'm kind of glad. It's not easy being the strong one.

Monsieur Dandurand takes a seat across from us, next to the nosy lady. He laces his fingers together on his lap and eyes the newspaper on the table between us, but he doesn't pick it up.

Colette has dozed off; her chin is poking into the back of my arm. I don't have the heart to push her away. Hôtel Dieu is French for God's Hotel. It's a terrible name for a hospital. If God had a hotel, I hope it would be a lot nicer than this. It would smell of coconut oil or roses, not pee and antiseptic. There'd be angels singing instead of machines beeping. And Mom…well, why did God let her get caught under the garage door in the first place? Father Lanctot says God has a plan for us, but I can't believe God would want this to happen to Mom.

I keep my eyes on the metal doors. More people go in than come out, and the ones who come out look grim and tired. Only one, a nurse with a tiny diamond stud in her nose, smiles at me.

"Girls!" I hear Dad's voice before I see him.

The nurse who tried to stop him before hears him too, because she looks up from behind the registration desk and scowls.

Maybe it's the fluorescent lighting, but I've never noticed before how big the bags under Dad's eyes are or how his sideburns are speckled with gray.

"Léonard," Dad says to Monsieur Dandurand. "You're still here."

"I wanted to keep an eye on the girls. And hear how Thérèse is."

"That's awfully kind of you," Dad says.

Monsieur Dandurand shrugs. "Whatever I can do to help."

The nosy lady peers over the top of her book and checks Dad out. There doesn't seem to be anything wrong with her. Maybe she sits in the ER waiting room all day, listening in on other people's conversations. I try glaring at her, but that's the one thing she doesn't seem to notice.

Colette uncurls herself and rubs her eyes. She's not leaning on me now, but I can still feel her weight on my arm. "How's Mom?" she asks.

Dad kneels on the floor in front of us. "The neuro-surgeon just finished examining her. He can't tell for sure yet how seriously she's injured." Dad sucks in his breath. "She still has no feeling below the waist. But that could be temporary. When the inflammation subsides, she may get sensation back. That's what we're hoping for. And we have to remember, things could have been a lot worse." He sucks in his breath again. "We could have lost her."

Dad's words hang in the air. *We could have lost her.* I know everybody has to die one day, but somehow, this is the first time I've ever really understood that one day Mom will die, and Dad too. The thought makes me go panicky inside. I feel little and lost and like I want to run away, but there's no place to go. How will Colette and I ever manage without them? I push the thought away. It's too sad and scary to imagine a world without my parents in it.

But at least now we know something. And we have something to hope for.

Colette is rocking again. "What's going to happen?" she cries out. "Is Mom going to be okay—or is she going to be a cripple for the rest of her life?"

Dad shakes his head. I dig my nails into the armrest. The nosy lady sighs.

Eight

I won't take my eyes off Mom. Even if I'm having trouble keeping them open. No way. I'm watching Mom's sleeping face and the scratchy yellow blanket that covers her lower body. I keep hoping for some sign of movement—anything—but there is none.

One of us has been with her round the clock since the accident happened two days ago. I came up with the idea of making a schedule. I stuck it on the refrigerator, next to a photo of Mom and Dad posing by the waterfall, their faces young and happy-looking. Colette is coming by bus to relieve me, and Dad will take over from her after he closes the shop. Clara is working extra hours, so that helps too.

There's a ripple in the blanket and I nearly call out, but it's just a breeze coming in through the window.

My stomach is rumbling—all I had for breakfast was an Egg McMuffin—but I won't let myself sleep or eat or even pee. All I want to do is be here at Mom's bedside. Part of me hopes that by keeping such close watch over her I'll help make her better.

Hope. It's what we've been living on since Sunday. We're breathing, eating, even dreaming hope. Hope is light and airy, hope feels kind, but there are heavier, darker, unkind thoughts and feelings in me too. Like this one: Mom could be paraplegic—paralyzed from the waist down—for the rest of her life. She might never walk again, never hike, or even use the bathroom on her own. She might have to spend the rest of her life in a wheelchair. Like Marco Leblanc. And then what will happen to us?

Mom's on an intravenous muscle relaxant that makes her sleepy. The doctors stapled up the wound on her lower back where the door hit. "There's no need for painkillers," the neurosurgeon explained to us, "since she can't feel the pain. For now."

"Are you saying it would be a good thing if she felt pain?" Dad asked.

"Exactly."

I keep thinking about that. How pain's something we all fear and try to avoid, and now we're hoping, praying even, for Mom to feel pain.

The doctor said the first few days following a spinal-cord injury are critical.

But how many days is a few? It's already Tuesday. I count out the days on my fingers. Sunday, Monday, Tuesday. But if I count from the time of the accident, well then, it's just two days. A few days must be more than two.

The hospital room smells of cut flowers. Everyone has sent bouquets—old friends, longtime customers, the Dandurands, even the mayor and his wife. I notice the water in one of the vases is turning brown. I should change it, but that would mean leaving Mom. And I won't—not even for the time it would take to flush the old water down the toilet.

I hear Colette's voice from down the hall. She must be saying hi to everyone in the ICU. A moment later, she bursts into Mom's room. "How is she?"

"The same."

Colette slides off her backpack and dumps it at the bottom of Mom's bed, near her feet. Then Colette leans over to take out something she's wrapped in a dish towel. It's the crucifix Mom wanted to hang in the dining room.

The one Dad said made him lose his appetite. I guess Mom never got around to finding another spot for it.

"Mom'll like that," I say, and Colette's face brightens. "Leave it on her nightstand so she'll see it when she wakes up."

"I've got a better idea." Colette reaches inside the backpack and fishes out a hammer and a small folded piece of paper. A nail falls out, landing somewhere on the yellow blanket.

"You can't do that!" I hiss.

"Oh yes I can."

"Colette!"

"Saint Ani strikes again," Colette mutters.

"Don't call me that."

Colette sighs. She finds the nail, wraps it back inside the paper and stashes it together with the hammer under Mom's blanket. Colette is hoping I'll forget about her plan.

"Put the hammer back in your backpack," I tell Colette. "And the nail too."

She shakes her head.

When Colette lifts the edge of the blanket, we see Mom's feet. They look pale and veiny and both her baby toes are calloused, probably from hiking. Colette runs her hand over one of Mom's feet. I know she is watching for some sign that Mom can feel her. But nothing registers.

"I'll take the hammer home," I tell Colette. I use my firmest voice—the one Colette sometimes listens to.

"No way," Colette says. "I want to hang the crucifix right there." She fixes her eyes on the wall opposite Mom's bed.

"You could get in a lot of trouble, for...for"—I search for the right words, something that will scare Colette into giving me the hammer—"for defacing public property."

I try to reach under the blanket and grab the hammer, but Colette pushes me away.

"Okay, then. I give up. But I don't want to be here when you do it. I'm going home to sleep. Phone right away if there's news. Any news at all." I lean over to kiss Mom goodbye. Her breath smells sour and her beautiful hair is so greasy it looks like it's glued to her head.

"Are you gonna be all right?" I ask Colette. Sitting still for six hours is about the hardest thing you can ask Colette to do. "Did you bring something to do—and something to eat?"

"I've got an *Elle* magazine. And Dad gave me money for the cafeteria. Look, I'm sorry I called you Saint Ani before. It's just...just...you're always acting so...well, so good. You make me feel like I'm bad." Colette makes a strange blubbering noise, something between a sneeze and a sob. "The thing is"—Colette can hardly get the words out now—"I am bad. I know I am. I shouldn't have left Mom alone in the shop. I was being selfish."

I know Colette wants me to tell her Mom's accident wasn't her fault, that Mom is going to be okay, that she'll regain movement in her legs and that all our lives will go back to what they were like before.

But right now, I can't give Colette what she wants. Right now, I'm too sad and too drained to be anyone's big sister. And I'm bone tired of always having to do the right thing, and say the right thing, and look after Colette and her special needs and her feelings.

"You know, Colette, everything isn't always about you. This"—for a second, my hands fly up into the air—"this is about Mom. She's the one who may never be able to walk again. Not you."

Colette's mouth forms an O. She reaches for my hand, but I shake it away. I don't care if I've let Colette down or hurt her feelings. I've had it with caring, with being good. It's too much work.

There is a knock at the door. I figure it's a doctor or a nurse. I hope whoever it is hasn't heard us arguing.

Someone clears his throat. "May I come in?" a man's voice asks.

A doctor or a nurse wouldn't bother asking.

The man isn't wearing scrubs and he doesn't have a stethoscope around his neck. He has thick dark hair. And then I realize how I know him. It's the handsome priest who was talking to Mom outside the shop, the one who was assisting Father Lanctot at Sunday Mass. Only he isn't wearing his priest's collar now.

"I came as soon as I could," he says as he walks into the room. Then he stops to introduce himself. "I'm Father Francoeur. Your mom and I knew each other when we were kids. I saw you at church," he says when our eyes meet. "It's uncanny how much you look like she did then."

"It's good of you to come," I say.

Colette shoots me a look. I know I sound prissy, but I can't help it. I'm not used to making conversation with priests.

I extend my hand. My cheeks are hot. I feel his eyes land on my earrings—the ones with the crosses. I've worn them every day since the accident. I even wear them in the shower and when I go to sleep. "I'm Ani. This is my sister Colette."

Father Francoeur clasps my hands and then Colette's. His fingers feel dry and cool. He steps closer to Mom's bedside. I watch him watching Mom's face. He looks as

peaceful as she does. Then he closes his eyes. I wonder if
he's remembering back to when he and Mom were kids.
I wonder what kind of stuff they used to do together.

Father Francoeur opens his eyes. "The Lord cured
the paralytic woman, for she had faith." His voice is
gentle and calm. I wonder if that's something he learned
at seminary school—or if having that kind of voice is
a prerequisite for getting in. Then he closes his eyes again.
I know it's because he's praying now. I close my eyes too.

"Where's your priest's collar?" Colette asks Father
Francoeur.

"Colette!" I say. "Can't you see Father Francoeur is
praying?"

When Father Francoeur smiles, I can suddenly
picture him as a teenager. I'll bet he was a little nerdy
but already handsome. There's a dimple in his chin.
"Sometimes that collar gets a little tight around my neck.
Besides, I'm here today as a friend, not as a priest."

Though we have all been whispering, Mom is waking
up. Her eyelids have begun to flutter. If only her legs and
feet would flutter too!

"My girls!" she says, smiling when she sees us. Her
voice is so weak we have to lean in to hear her. "Emil!"

His first name is Emil.

Mom tries to use her elbows to hoist herself up, but even that one simple movement is too much for her.

Colette slides her arm behind Mom's back and props her up a little. I press the button that raises the head of the bed.

Mom nods. I think she's too tired to thank us.

Now Mom reaches for Father Francoeur's hand, using it to pull herself up a little higher. "Emil," she says, looking right at him. "I have to get out of here."

"Thérèse, it isn't time yet for that," he tells her. "But soon. When you are a little stronger."

"You don't understand," Mom says, and for the first time since the accident, she is crying. Fat round tears dribble down her cheeks. "I need to go to the basilica. I need to ask for Sainte Anne's intercession."

Nine

Emil—Father Francoeur—doesn't want to stay too long. He says he's afraid of tiring Mom out and that she needs all the rest she can get. I'm glad he's there. Even his short visit has changed the mood in the hospital room. It's calmer now, and the electricity that was in the air when Colette and I were arguing is gone.

When Father Francoeur finds out I'm taking the bus back to Ste-Anne-de-Beaupré, he offers to drive me. "It's the least I can do. Besides, I'm afraid that after being up all night you'll fall asleep on the bus and miss your stop. You might wake up in Baie-Saint-Paul! No, no, we can't have that."

Mom doesn't like the idea. "Emil, you must have church business here in Quebec City. And Ani will be fine on the bus, won't you, dear?"

But Father Francoeur insists. "I need to get back to town. Besides, I'd enjoy the company."

Mom's too weak to argue.

"I almost forgot," Father Francoeur says, reaching into his jacket pocket, "I brought you something." It's a miniature Bible, the kind you need a magnifying glass to read. We carry them at Saintly Souvenirs, but this one looks ancient; the edges of its black cover are frayed.

"Emil," Mom says, her voice cracking a little, "is that the one I gave you?"

"The very one. I've kept it with me always. I even took it to Africa. Now it's time to return it."

He hands Mom the tiny Bible. She leafs through the pages, so thin they are almost transparent, then presses it to her heart. "I can't believe you kept it all this time."

Father Francoeur smiles. "That Bible," he says, "was my favorite souvenir." The way he drags out each syllable makes me think about what the word *souvenir* means in French—a memory. It's weird knowing Mom has shared memories with this man, who, until Colette and I saw him on Avenue Royale two weeks ago, we never knew existed.

By the time Father Francoeur and I are ready to go, Mom's chin has dropped to her chest. She has dozed off, the tiny Bible still pressed to her heart.

I'm a little shocked when Father Francoeur leans over and strokes Mom's hair. The gesture seems so…so intimate. Especially for a priest. I feel more comfortable when, before we leave Mom's room, he makes the sign of the cross and says a prayer for her. "In the name of the Father, the Son and the Holy Spirit, I bless you and I absolve you from your sins." Mom sighs in her sleep.

All I can think is: what sins? Mom's always kind to everyone. Sure, she can be strict, but I don't think I've ever heard her shout or get angry or swear. Somehow, that makes what's happened to her even worse, even more senseless.

On our way out, Father Francoeur pats Colette's shoulder. "Pray for her," he whispers.

Colette's eyes meet mine, but she doesn't say anything—or roll her eyes.

Almost as soon as we leave Mom's room, some of my tiredness begins to lift. I even feel kind of proud to be walking down the hallway and taking the elevator with Father Francoeur. Several women—one is a doctor—turn to look when he goes by, though he doesn't seem to notice. I wonder how they'd feel if they knew they were checking out a priest.

Father Francoeur's car is parked in the hospital lot, and he lets me in first, the way Dad does for Mom on her birthday or when they're going out on one of their Friday night "dates." How long, I wonder, will it be till Mom and Dad have another date? And will Mom have to be transported in a wheelchair?

Father Francoeur's car has that plasticky new-car smell. Mom says the smell comes from toxic chemicals, so I lower my window, just in case.

I wonder if the car—a Toyota—belongs to the church. Aren't priests supposed to take a vow of poverty? If Colette was here, she'd ask. One advantage to having Colette for a sister is I find out a lot of interesting stuff without having to be the one asking embarrassing questions.

Father Francoeur must've forgotten to turn off the radio, because it starts to blare when he puts the key in the ignition. "We were born, born to be wi-i-i-ld!" some guy half sings, half screams.

"Oops," Father Francoeur says as he hits the Off button. He must know I'm surprised, because he says, "Hey, just because I'm a priest doesn't mean I don't like rock music. Especially Canadian rock."

He waits for me to buckle up before he backs out of the parking spot. "So tell me, Ani"—I can feel his eyes on my face—"how are you doing?"

It isn't until he asks that I realize I've been so worried about Mom these last few days I haven't thought much about my other emotions. And now, I'm not sure where to begin. I'm sad. I'm angry. I'm hopeful. I'm not sure hope can help. But for some reason I don't quite understand, I feel like I can say all that to Father Francoeur—maybe because he's a priest, and because he's Mom's old friend, and because when he's alone in his car he listens to rock and roll.

I run my hands over my thighs and sigh. Even sighing feels good. It's as if I haven't really breathed since Sunday. "To tell you the truth, I don't even know how I'm doing."

Father Francoeur nods. He's thinking about what I just said. "You haven't had much time to process what's happened." The way he says it—like he understands exactly what I mean—makes me want to tell him more.

"I'm scared," I say in a small voice.

"Of course you are. And that's okay." Father Francoeur slips one hand off the wheel and gives my hand a squeeze. There are freckles on the back of his hand. I remember how he stroked Mom's hair before and, though it doesn't make sense, for a second I'm jealous. "Tell me what you're scared of."

"I'm scared"—I can feel my top lip quiver—"Mom'll be a paraplegic."

"Being scared is normal in a situation like this," Father Francoeur says. "Faith can help us overcome our fears."

"Do you think if I have faith—if I pray hard enough—that Mom will walk again?"

We've come to a stop sign and now Father Francoeur is looking at his hands. "Faith," he says slowly, "is believing God knows best. Even if we don't always understand His ways."

Father Francoeur must know that's not the answer I wanted. "I want a guarantee…," I say, hesitating a little before I go on, "that everything's is going to be all right."

"That's just it," Father Francoeur says, smiling. "Everything is going to be all right. No matter what happens."

"But Mom could end up like Marco Leblanc."

Father Francoeur turns to look at me. "Marco Leblanc? Now that's a name I haven't heard in a long time. I thought Marco left Ste-Anne-de-Beaupré years ago. After the accident."

"He lives across the street from us."

"He does? Well then, I'd better go and see him one of these days."

"Were you and Marco Leblanc friends?"

"We were all friends. In those days, no one got left out."

We drive along in silence for a while. The sky is as blue as the Saint Lawrence River in La Malbaie, where it widens to meet up with the Atlantic Ocean. Somehow, it feels wrong for the sky to be so blue when Mom is trapped in a hospital bed.

"It feels like it should be a gray day, doesn't it? A day with giant storm clouds?"

I turn to look at Father Francoeur when he says that. That was spooky. It's as if he read my thoughts. The only other person that ever happens with is Colette...

Colette. By now, she's probably hammered the nail into the wall and hung up the crucifix. I wonder if the nurses came running when they heard the banging. She should have let me take the hammer home. But *should* doesn't mean much to Colette. And though she frustrates me more than anyone else on earth, I know she has a good heart. A pure heart.

All Colette wanted was for Mom to see that crucifix when she woke up. Again I get the feeling I was too hard on Colette. I shouldn't have shouted at her. I should have been more sympathetic when she told me she felt responsible for Mom's accident. I should be a better person. It's just that sometimes being better feels like such hard work.

"Did you hear me shouting at Colette before?" I hope Father Francoeur will say he didn't.

"I wouldn't call it shouting. But yes, I heard you raise your voice with Colette. You're the big sister, aren't you?"

"Uh-huh."

"That must be hard sometimes. Especially in times like these when you're under tremendous stress."

"She's got ADHD. That makes it even harder." For a moment, I feel guilty for mentioning Colette's condition. It's not something we usually talk about with other people. Mom thinks people have prejudices against kids with learning disabilities. She says it's better they get to know Colette and appreciate her for who she is before we tell them she has ADHD.

"I wondered about that," Father Francoeur says. "She's certainly high-energy. She reminds me of a puppy. You're more like a colt."

A colt. I'm trying to decide whether that's a compliment. "Can I ask you something?"

Father Francoeur nods. "Anything."

I take a deep breath. "Do you ever feel angry? Or sad?" I pause for a moment. "Or jealous?"

When Father Francoeur chuckles, the sound fills the whole car, and for some reason, my body feels lighter than it's felt all day, lighter than it's felt since Mom's accident.

"Of course I do. I sometimes feel angry and sad and jealous. And sometimes all three at the same time."

"You do?" I feel as if Father Francoeur has just confessed to being a serial killer. "But you're a priest."

"I'm also a human being. Which, in the end, probably makes me a better priest."

"Can I ask you something else?"

"Fire away."

"This might sound weird, but is it hard for you to be good? Or does it come...naturally?"

Father Francoeur chuckles again. "So you think I'm a good person, do you?"

"Well, you're a priest. Priests have to be good." As soon as I say that, I realize how dumb I must sound. Everyone knows there are priests who abuse kids. "Or else they shouldn't be priests."

"I have to work at being good," Father Francoeur says. "I'd say that's the human condition—whether or not you're a priest."

I like that. The human condition. So maybe I'm not as bad as I thought. "Can I ask you one more thing?"

"Wasn't that the one more thing?"

"I thought of another one."

"Well, go ahead. You know, Ani, I like your questions. They show you're a searcher."

I like the idea of being a searcher too. It makes it easier for me to ask my next question. "What was Mom like before—when you knew her?" I think about the old pictures I've seen of Mom. In them, she hardly ever looks directly at the camera.

Father Francoeur lifts one hand to his neck as if he wants to adjust his priest's collar, only when he realizes he isn't wearing the collar, he puts his hand back on the wheel.

"She was…she was beautiful and fun…and a little… well, a little wild."

"Wild? You've got to be kidding. Not my mom." I'm thinking how Father Francoeur's definition of wild is probably skipping church on Sunday or forgetting to say your prayers before you go to bed.

"Yes, your mom. She's the one who taught me how to smoke."

"No way. Mom never smoked."

Father Francoeur rubs his mouth. I think he's smiling underneath. "Oops," he says. "I guess that was supposed to be a secret."

"Mom smoked?" I can't picture it. "Where? Where did you guys used to go to smoke?" I think about how some of the kids from school smoke on the bench outside the McDonald's.

"Behind the Scala Santa. She knew how to make smoke rings. I could never do it."

"The Scala Santa?" The Scala Santa is an old wooden chapel across the road from the basilica. It's got holy stairs—that's what Scala Santa means—that are supposed to represent Jesus' agony before the crucifixion. The Scala Santa is one of the holiest places in town.

"But she had a spiritual side too. When I made the decision to enroll in the seminary, she was the most supportive of all our friends. Even though it was hard for her."

I'm still trying to picture Mom smoking behind the Scala Santa—Mom being wild. But in my mind, all I can see is Mom showing me a new crucifix, or coming in from a hike with her cheeks flushed, or—and this is the picture I wish I didn't have to see—using her elbows to try to pull herself up in her hospital bed. No, I just can't see Mom acting wild.

The next thought that goes through my head takes me a little by surprise. I'm thinking that if Mom ever did act wild—if she really did blow smoke rings behind the Scala Santa—well then, I'm glad.

Jen

Father Francoeur scribbles his phone number on a slip of paper (somehow I expected a priest to have neater handwriting), folds it in two and hands it to me. "Call me," he says, "the next time you go see her, and if I can, I'll give you a ride. In the mean time, be gentle with yourself. And pray. I'll be praying too—for all of you."

I tell Father Francoeur he can leave me at the basilica. I should stop at Saintly Souvenirs, but I'm not sure how Dad would feel about my getting a lift home from Father Francoeur. I wonder if Dad knows Mom used to smoke and that she and Father Francoeur hung out together.

Father Francoeur gives my hand another squeeze before we say goodbye. This time, I squeeze back. I can't help thinking again how handsome he is. I like his profile best. His nose is straight and not too long, and his nostrils flare a little. From the side, his face looks chiseled, as if someone had sculpted him from marble.

When Father Francoeur drops me off and I'm standing alone on Avenue Royale, I start feeling sad and overwhelmed and tired all over again. I need to sleep. I'll feel better once I get some rest. First I should see how Dad and Clara are managing at the shop. But the idea of facing Dad and Clara makes me feel even more tired. So tired I could collapse here on the sidewalk—and never get up. If Father Francoeur knew how I was feeling right now, what would he say?

He'd tell me to go to the basilica. Even just for a few minutes—to help me find my calm place. So that's what I do.

Usually, no matter what time I go, there's always someone there, kneeling in one of the pews, palms pressed together, whispering a prayer. But today, for the first time ever, I am alone. I have the entire basilica to myself.

I go straight to our pew.

I can practically feel the holiness soaking into my pores. Father Francoeur would be impressed if he knew. There I go again—thinking of him.

I bring my thoughts back to the Lord and to Mom. After all, that's why I'm here. "Please, Lord," I say as I kneel down, "please let Mom walk again. And give us the strength we need to help her."

Then instead of leaving, I stay a few more minutes. I'm not praying now; I'm just letting the sacred air fill me up. Something tells me I'm going to need it.

֍

Clara is straightening the crucifixes on the wall behind the cash register. But she rushes over when I come in. "Is there any news?" I can see the worry in her eyes.

Because it helped when Father Francoeur squeezed my hand, I pat Clara's elbow. "No news. But we have to hope—and pray. Where's my dad?"

"He said he had things to do at home." Clara's eyes are getting moist. I know it's because she feels responsible for Mom's accident too. If she'd been able to fix the alarm or if she hadn't freaked out, Mom would never have left the picnic. But there's no point in going over all the what-ifs.

I wonder whether Father Francoeur would say Mom's accident was God's will. Now I'm sorry I didn't ask him that when we were in the car. Maybe he thinks all bad things that happen are God's will—poverty and home-lessness and tsunamis and war. Maybe he thinks they're some kind of test.

"It wasn't your fault," I tell Clara.

I can tell from the look in her eyes she doesn't believe me.

The tiredness comes back as I trudge along Avenue Royale toward our house. I hear hammering from down the street. What's going on? For as long as I can remember, Mom has been bugging Dad to repair the wood fence around our property. Maybe he's finally getting around to it. Maybe it's his way of telling Mom how bad he feels about the accident.

"Dad!" I call out. "I'm home!"

"Ani!" he calls back. "I just phoned your sister. She says there's still no change. Come see what I've been up to!" His voice sounds proud. I must be right about the fence. It's something he can do for Mom while she is trapped in the hospital. Though I'm tired, I speed up. I feel as if a repaired and freshly painted fence will make me feel better too.

But the wobbly fence posts are still wobbly and the one that is missing—knocked out during a snowstorm—is still missing. Dad is hard at work all right, but on another project altogether.

He's building a wheelchair ramp. It's made of plywood and it starts at our front door and goes almost to our gravel driveway. Dad is on his hands and knees, and I see giant sweat stains on his T-shirt. There's a nail between his lips.

The wheelchair ramp is the ugliest thing I've ever seen.

Dad's nose is sunburned and his forehead is shiny with sweat. If Mom were here, she'd have reminded him to use sunscreen. Who's going to take care of all that now?

"What do you think?" Dad asks, watching my face for my reaction.

That's when I start to bawl.

Dad throws up his arms. The nail falls out of his mouth and I hear it rolling along the ramp. "I don't understand," he says. "It's for her. For your mom. For when she comes home."

As if I couldn't figure that out. "Maybe she won't need it," I manage to say between sobs.

Dad rushes over to where I'm standing and tries to wrap his arms around my shoulders. But he is making me sweaty too, and I push him away. I haven't cried since the accident and now I can't stop.

"Ani," Dad says, putting his fingers under my chin and lifting my face so he can look into my eyes, "I know this is hard. But we have to start dealing with it."

I try pushing him away again, but Dad keeps looking into my eyes and talking to me in his steady voice. "Your mother is going to need a wheelchair to get around. Maybe just for a while, maybe forever. The doctor thinks there is very little chance she will regain movement in her lower body." This time Dad's voice breaks and I'm the one who has to hug him—sweaty T-shirt and all.

"Maybe," I whisper, and my voice is hoarse from crying, "maybe there'll be a miracle. If we pray."

I feel Dad's shoulders tense up.

There is balled-up Kleenex in my pocket. I hand a piece to Dad. He blows his nose so loud he sounds like a loon.

I hear a creaking noise from the balcony across the street. It bothers me to know Marco Leblanc has been watching us from his blackbird's nest—that he's seen me crying and Dad and me hugging each other. Marco will know from the wheelchair ramp Dad is building that something bad has happened.

This town is way too small for me.

Eleven

There are a couple of things I really want to know, but I'm too embarrassed to ask anybody. The first is this: If Mom stays paralyzed, how will she go to the bathroom? In the hospital these last two weeks, she's been hooked up to a catheter that's attached to a thick plastic bag where her pee collects. I don't know how the other part works. And I don't dare ask. What worries me is how it's going to work at home. Will one of us have to bring her to the bathroom—and will we have to wipe her bum the way she did ours when we were babies? Because if we do, I'm not sure I can handle it. Wiping a one-year-old's bum is one thing, but wiping your mother's…no, as much as I love Mom and as much as I want to be able to do the right thing, I don't think I can do it.

The other thing I'm wondering about is whether Mom and Dad will still be able to have sex. Though the idea of them doing it has always grossed me out, the idea of them not being able to do it ever again makes me even more upset. I mean, in a loving relationship, sex is supposed to strengthen the bond between two people. At least that's what they told us in Moral and Religious Ed, and it made sense—well, sort of, anyhow. So if Mom and Dad can't have sex anymore—and how could they if Mom is paralyzed below the waist?—what's going to happen to their bond? Maybe Dad'll want to leave Mom for somebody healthier. And then what would happen to us?

I could look online for answers, but to be honest, I'm afraid of what I'll find if I google *paraplegics + bodily wastes*, or *paraplegics + sex*. There's so much sick stuff on the web, and if the search leads me to some paraplegic porn site, I swear I'll be scarred for life.

No, there's an easier way to find out.

I'll get Colette to ask.

Too bad she's sleeping.

Except for when she was on Ritalin, Colette has always been a way better sleeper than me. Maybe it's because she uses up so much energy fidgeting and yakking all day. At night, all she has to do is put her cheek on the pillow and she's out cold.

Not me. Sleep's always been a struggle for me. Especially if there's something on my mind—the way there is tonight.

I try telling my body to relax, but my body isn't taking orders. I try counting the glow-in-the-dark stars Colette and I stuck on the ceiling in our bedroom, but that doesn't help either. I try focusing on the music the crickets are making outside, but instead, I think I hear the creak of Marco Leblanc's wheelchair. Maybe he's as bad a sleeper as I am.

Colette sighs. This could be my chance. "Are you awake?" I whisper.

Colette doesn't answer. So I lie there a little longer, to see if she wakes up on her own. Our bedroom door is half open and I see a pair of yellow eyes glowing in the dark. I move over to the side of my bed and tap the spot next to me. Eeyore jumps up, landing with a soft thud. I stroke the fur behind his ears the way he likes. Sometimes, petting Eeyore helps me fall asleep.

It's Eeyore's purring that wakes Colette up. She shifts on her bed, then yawns. "What are you doing to that cat?" she asks, her voice thick with sleep.

"Nothing. Just petting him. I can't sleep."

"Did you try counting the stars?"

"It didn't help."

"Do you want me to make you a cup of warm milk?"

I know Colette means it. That she'd actually get up and warm up some milk for me. And because Mom got rid of the microwave—she thinks microwaves give off dangerous electrical waves—Colette would have stood by the stove and warmed the milk in a small pot. "Nah, but thanks for offering."

I hear Colette shift onto her other side. "Colette—"

"Uh-huh."

"There's some stuff I'm wondering about. About Mom." I'm almost too shy to talk about it.

"Is it about sex?"

I'm glad Colette said the word, not me. And she didn't seem the least bit embarrassed about it either. "Well, yeah, and about going to the bathroom. How's that gonna work exactly?"

"I think she'll have to keep wearing a diaper. You know—for number two's. And I'm pretty sure she'll still have the catheter for peeing."

"Mom wears a diaper?"

"You haven't noticed?"

94

"I guess not. I didn't really think about it till now." I suck in my breath. "Will we have to wipe her? Or change the diaper?"

"She changed plenty of ours."

"Yeah, but we were babies. Our poops were baby-size."

"We can't expect Dad to do everything," Colette says. I know she's right. "The diapers might just be temporary," Colette continues. "I read online that, over time, people who are paraplegic get to recognize the rhythms of their bodies. She'll be able to tell us when she has to go. Then one of us will have to help her onto the toilet."

"And off," I add, trying to picture how it'll work.

After that, neither of us says anything for a while. The Saint Anne nightlight on the bottom of the wall opposite our beds casts a pale white light.

Colette yawns again, and now I yawn too. It feels like some of the tension from not sleeping is beginning to drain out of me. Maybe I'll be able to doze off after all.

I'm turning my pillow over when Colette starts talking again. "I'm pretty sure they can still have sex." She pauses for a moment as if she's thinking of something. "I'll ask Dad if you want."

"You'd ask him that?"

"Sure, why not? Or we could ask the social worker at the hospital. She's supposed to help us make the transition when Mom comes home. Besides, there's more to sex than—you know—intercourse."

I can feel my ears heat up. I can't believe Colette just used the word *intercourse*. Eeyore jumps down to the floor. I think he's embarrassed too.

"How do you know?" It bothers me that Colette is so comfortable talking about sex. It should be the other way around. After all, I'm the big sister.

Colette giggles in the darkness. "I know because."

I sit up in my bed. So much for dozing off. "Because what?"

"Because I'm learning."

"You mean from Moral and Religious Ed?"

"No, not from MRE." Colette giggles again.

"From what then?"

At first, Colette won't tell me.

"Colette!"

"From Maxim. We're going out. Well, sort of."

I can't believe Colette has kept a secret from me. Colette can't keep secrets. I think it's part of her condition. And I can't believe Colette and Maxim have been fooling around! It's bad enough that Josianne and Armand can't keep their hands off each other. It's like everyone is turning into some kind of sex maniac. Everyone except me.

Good Catholics are supposed to wait until they're married to have sex. I know not everybody follows that rule, but I want to. Besides, maybe by the time I get married, my breasts'll be bigger, and the idea of letting a boy see me naked won't seem so awful. "When do you see him?" It's all I can manage to say.

"He comes by sometimes. When you're at the hospital and Dad's at the store."

I look around our room. Has Colette brought him here? It doesn't seem right that I didn't know.

"You're not supposed to have sex before marriage," I say into the dark, but already I know that Colette won't care. She's as interested in *supposed to* as she is in *should*.

"We're not having sex. Not exactly. We're just having fun. Anyway, everyone has sex before marriage." Colette makes it sound like she's talking about what we're going to have for breakfast.

"That's not true. Not everyone."

"Mom did."

Now Colette has gone too far. I won't let her say something like that about Mom. "No, she didn't," I say, and for a second I wonder if I'm talking so loud I might wake Dad up. "Mom's a good Catholic. She waited till her wedding night. I'm sure she did."

When Colette laughs, I know she's laughing at me. "You don't really believe that, do you?"

I don't say anything. I wish I'd never started this dumb conversation.

"Well, why do you think she and dad got married when she was just eighteen?"

I cross my arms over my chest. "Because they loved each other."

"Sure they loved each other. But"—Colette lowers her voice—"I'll bet you that wasn't the only reason."

There's really only one thing I'm sure of now: I'm never going to fall asleep tonight.

Twelve

I'm having my bowl of organic muesli (no artificial sweeteners) on the back porch when I notice the ladybug. She's on her back on the edge of the wrought-iron table across from me. Are they all females? I wonder. Why else would people call them ladybugs? I wonder how she got stuck. Maybe she fell down from somewhere up in our old oak tree and landed that way. Or maybe a gust of wind blew her over. Her tiny legs—or whatever you call what insects use to get around—are flailing in the air. Ladybugs have wings too, but maybe they don't work when they're upside down.

I want to help her out and turn her right side up, but I'm afraid if I touch her, I might squash her. I could try using the end of my spoon, but I'd have to be careful not to poke her, and besides, my spoon's got milk on it. So I move my chair a little closer and lean over so I can blow on her.

I take a breath and blow, but not too hard. I'm thinking of the wolf in "The Three Little Pigs"—and of how, in Genesis, God gave man life by breathing into him. The wolf used his breath to destroy the houses of the first two pigs. God used his for creation.

It's only when the ladybug flips over that I realize she's one of those rare orange ladybugs. The kind Tante Hélène spotted that day we went on the picnic. The day of Mom's accident. Somehow, starting my morning off with this orange ladybug and being able to turn her right side up with my breath feels like a good sign. It also feels like a good sign when a moment later she flies off, leaving only the memory of her bright orange shell behind.

৩৩

Mom's coming home. It's been almost three weeks since the accident. The doctors and physiotherapists at the hospital have done everything they can, and now, because the hospital is so overcrowded, they need her bed for another patient. Mom is still paralyzed from the waist down.

Dad has put in a wheelchair ramp in front of Saintly Souvenirs too. He says he doesn't know why he never thought of it before. Having the ramp will be good for business, and it'll make things easier when, eventually, Mom starts doing some work in the shop.

The three of us go to pick Mom up. Dad has rented a collapsible metal ramp. That way Mom can stay in her wheelchair and we can load her right into the back of the van.

She's sitting in her wheelchair when we come, her suitcase on her lap. Carole Tremblay, the social worker assigned to Mom's case, is with her. "We'll talk next week," Carole tells Mom, leaning down to give her a big hug. "You keep your chin up, okay, Thérèse?"

Mom pats Carole's back. "I hope your son gets over that bronchitis soon," Mom tells her. It's so like Mom to know Carole's son has bronchitis. Maybe Mom should've been a social worker.

Carole shakes Dad's hand. "One day at a time," she tells him, "and remember"—now Carole turns to Colette and me too—"your mom is still the same person she was before the accident."

Colette has grabbed the rubber handles on the back of Mom's wheelchair. "Of course she is," she says.

But as Colette wheels Mom down the hospital hallway, with Dad and me on either side, it feels to me like Mom isn't at all the same person. My mom loved to hike in the woods and bicycle even in the pouring rain. My mom practically flew down the staircase in our house. My mom sang while she scrubbed the kitchen floor. What if this mom can never do any of those things again?

When I hit the Down button for the elevator, I see Carole is still in the doorway to Mom's room, watching us.

෧෨

Dad has made Mom's favorite—chicken salad with cut-up apples in it—for lunch. Colette picked black-eyed Susans and I helped her arrange them in an old milk jug that we put out on the dining-room table. Colette wanted to make a banner, but I told her that would be overdoing it.

"The wheelchair ramp is going to make things much easier," Dad tells Mom once we've managed to get her into the back of the van.

The fence is a surprise. Dad spent most of Saturday repairing it, and on Sunday he gave it two coats of white paint.

"I want to stop at the basilica first," Mom says as we leave Quebec City and get onto the 138.

"Are you sure it can't wait till tomorrow?" Dad asks.

"I'm sure."

Dad sighs. "In that case, we'll stop at the basilica first."

We're not alone in the basilica today. There are several people in the pews, praying quietly. And there's a cleaning person mopping one of the side aisles.

Dad has come inside too. It's the first time I've seen him in the basilica, though I know he was here when he and Mom got married and, later, for my baptism and Colette's. He looks around as if he's afraid someone might jump out from behind a golden pillar and mug him, or worse, try to convert him. Colette is holding on to his hand.

"Except for the TV monitors," Dad whispers, looking up at the screens on either side of the altar and the ones behind the pews, "everything still looks the same in here."

Mom wants us to wheel her as close as we can get her to the Miraculous Statue of Saint Anne. It's a beautiful wooden statue painted gold. And there are real gems—amethysts, turquoises and corals—in Saint Anne's crown.

Dad brings Mom's wheelchair right up to the marble riser. "Close enough?" he asks her.

Mom nods. She drops her chin to her chest and begins to pray. She's whispering, and though I could try to listen, I take a few steps back. Mom needs some private time with Saint Anne.

I let my chin drop to my chest too. I want to pray. I want to pray harder than I've ever prayed. Please, Saint Anne, please, please, I beg of you, heal my good mother. Let her walk again. Please intercede on her behalf.

I close my eyes and press my palms so close together they burn.

I can just make out the hushed sound of Mom's whispering.

"All right," Mom says, "I'm ready to go home now."

Dad wheels her down the center aisle. When I catch up with Mom, I run my hand over her skirt, along where her thighs are. But she doesn't look up. Mom still can't feel a thing.

What was I expecting?

I know it doesn't make sense to feel disappointed, but I can't help it. And when we've left the basilica, we pass the statue of Saint Anne in the middle of the pond, I turn away so I won't have to look at the saint for whom

I am named. The saint who didn't come through when I needed her.

୫୭

I haven't seen Mom cry really hard since the accident. But she weeps when she sees the work Dad's done on the fence. "Oh, Robert!" she says, her voice cracking. "After all these years."

"I should have done it sooner," Dad whispers.

Mom doesn't say anything about the wheelchair ramp though. But she doesn't want us to help her. "I need to be able to do this myself," she says, gritting her teeth as she uses both arms to make the wheelchair move forward. The wheelchair pulls to the right, and I rush over to straighten it out. "Don't!" Mom tells me.

I turn to see if Marco Leblanc is watching from his balcony. But for once, he isn't there. His chrome weights glitter in the afternoon sun.

Thirteen

Dad's in the downstairs bathroom, helping Mom. Because the heat duct in our bedroom is over the bathroom, I can hear every word. Frankly, I wish I didn't have to. Mom and Dad haven't been getting along too well lately.

Truth is, Mom isn't getting along too well with anybody. The first two weeks after she got back from the hospital, her mood was pretty good. But last week the weather in our house turned cloudy. Mom's been getting crabbier and crabbier. Too crabby even to pray.

Last night, when Clara stopped by to say hi, Mom wouldn't come to the door, and she didn't want us to let Clara in either. "Tell her to go away," Mom whispered from her wheelchair, but I'm sure Clara heard.

It was the same the night before when Monsieur Dandurand brought us supper from L'Église. "How about you phone to thank the Dandurands?" Dad suggested afterward. "They've been awfully good to us."

"I'm not up to it," Mom said.

I offered to help her write a thank-you note instead. Colette said Mom could use her favorite stationery. (Not that writing a thank-you note on skull and cross-bones stationery would have been exactly appropriate.)

"No." Which I thought wasn't fair, considering how strict Mom was about training Colette and me to write thank-you notes. I'm afraid if Mom keeps pushing people away, her friends will stop trying to visit and Monsieur Dandurand will stop sending over free food.

"Let me do it myself," Mom is saying now, and I can hear her spitting into the sink. "I'm not a child, Robert. I can still brush my own teeth."

"I'm only trying to help," Dad says.

"If you want to help, just let me be. And don't come following me into the bathroom like a sad puppy."

"I'm sorry, Thérèse."

Mostly, I've been feeling bad for Mom, but I'm starting to feel bad for Dad now too. I know from the way he just said "I'm sorry" that his feelings are hurt. Mom shouldn't have said he was acting like a sad puppy. Even if he is acting like a sad puppy.

I'm beginning to think the accident has brought out another side of Mom's personality—a darker side. Before the accident, I don't think I ever heard Mom snap at anyone. And she used to care about washing her hair and looking nice. Mom hasn't let us wash her hair for a week; some days, she refuses to change out of her night-gown. ("Why do I need to get dressed? It's not as if I'm going anywhere!")

Is this angry, depressed woman my real mom, and was the other one, the mom from before the accident, an imposter? I wonder if, when people get sick or when they've been in some awful accident, they finally become who they really are. Or is it the other way around? Are we most ourselves when things are going fine? Or are we some combination of both?

Will the real Mom please stand up?

Maybe I should go downstairs and try to cheer Dad up, but I'm afraid I'll make things worse. Besides, what if Mom starts snapping at me next?

So I stay inside my room with the door shut. I'm sprawled on my bed, reading my copy of *The Life of Saint Anne*. It's written by a priest, so he only says good stuff about her. Mom gave me the book on my tenth birthday and I've kept it on my night table ever since. I liked it more when I was younger and I didn't have so many questions. Still, sometimes when I don't have much to do, I like flipping through the pages and reading bits and pieces of the story.

If I were Dad, I'd give Mom space, leave her alone the way she told him to, but I can tell from the way the floorboards are creaking that Dad is still down there, waiting outside the bathroom, trying to be helpful.

Mom's confined to the downstairs of our house. Dad took apart their bed and set it up in the living room. I helped him drag the velvet couch into the dining room. Now, the whole downstairs looks like we're preparing for a garage sale—or moving. Luckily the entrance to the downstairs bathroom is extra-wide so we didn't have to knock down part of a wall, so Mom can get into the bathroom in her wheelchair.

I hear Mom wheeling herself out of the bathroom. She still has trouble maneuvering the wheelchair around corners, but she gets angry if we try to help. "I need to be able to do this myself," she tells us, gritting her teeth from the effort.

Dad clears his throat. "Maybe we should think about washing your hair today, Thérèse," he says softly.

"Not today."

If it were me, I'd take that as a sign to end the conversation, but Dad doesn't. "Are you sure, Thérèse?"

"Yes, I'm sure."

Now I hear the sound of Dad flipping through a magazine. "Thér…," he says, but then he stops himself.

"What is it now?"

"Well, uh…I've been meaning to tell you about this article I read online. Some French neuroscientists are using electrical stimulation to get paralyzed rats to run again." Dad's voice sounds bright, but I can tell he's forcing it.

"Robert," Mom says his name like it's a warning.

"I thought it was a very hopeful study. And there's another group of researchers out in Alberta who've done some very interesting experiments with geckos. I thought you'd want to hear all about it."

"I don't. Geckos, for goodness sake."

"You know, Thérèse, things could be worse. You could've died when you got caught under the garage door."

"You're right," Mom says. "I could've died. But that isn't doing me much good now, is it?"

Dad doesn't say anything, but even from upstairs, I can feel the tension between them. It's traveling up the stairway and through the walls. "All right then,"

Dad says at last, "in that case, I think I'll go to my office and work on the accounts. Can I make you a cup of tea first, Thérèse?"

That breaks my heart—when he offers to make her a cup of tea. Even after she's been so mean to him.

If Mom answers, I can't hear it. I try to concentrate on *The Life of Saint Anne.* Ominous clouds are darkening the sky of Anne and Joachim's life. The priest who wrote the book liked using flowery language. Personally, I don't know why he didn't just say Anne and Joachim were having a hard time.

I hear Dad trudging up the stairs and the click of the light switch when he gets to his office, which is just down the hall from our bedroom.

Downstairs, Mom has started to cry. I think she's trying to say something between the sobs, but I can't make out the words. And I don't really want to.

I hear Dad breathing hard. He's upset too. Then I hear him trudge back down the stairs. I can tell from the number of steps that he's stopped halfway down. "What about the God you love so much?" Dad calls out. "Where is He now, when you really need Him?"

When, after a minute or two, Mom still doesn't answer, Dad goes back up to his office. I hear him sit down at his chair and sigh.

How come now, when both my parents are hurting and I should be trying to do something to help, all I really want to do is pull the sheets over my head and pretend none of this is happening?

※

"I'm home!" Colette calls out. I must've dozed off reading *The Life of Saint Anne*. If that priest had put in some of the more interesting parts of her life, maybe the book would've turned out better. I mean maybe Saint Anne didn't just automatically get over things after Joachim took off to the desert. Maybe they didn't talk for a while, or she got snappy with him. Maybe she had the hots for some other guy. And maybe, once she finally did get pregnant and gave birth to baby Mary, she discovered that being such an old mom was hard. Maybe taking care of the baby was so hard Saint Anne was glad to consecrate Mary to the church. These are all things the priest doesn't mention.

"I was over at Maxim's," Colette is telling Mom. I can imagine what Colette was doing at Maxim's house. Making out, I'll bet! I don't understand how Colette can act like sex is no big deal, when, for me, the whole idea is so…well, complicated. Part of me thinks sex is scary and sinful, and even a little gross—people rubbing the most private parts of their bodies together—but another part of me is curious about it. Not just because I wonder how it'll make my body feel, but also because I really do believe what they teach us in MRE: sex is a sacred mystery, kind of like religion itself.

I think my life would be easier if Colette and I had more in common than who our parents are.

I can hear Colette unzipping her backpack. "Tante Hélène made these brownies for you, Mom. There's ginger in them. She says ginger's good for your system."

I expect Mom to snap, but she doesn't. Maybe she snapped enough at Dad before and she's feeling mellower now.

It's probably safe to go downstairs. Besides, I wouldn't mind a brownie, even one that's good for my system. I hear Dad's office door opening too. Maybe he's also got a sudden brownie craving. Or maybe he's hoping Mom'll be nicer to him now.

"What's wrong with your chin?" I ask Colette when I see her. The skin on her chin is all red and bumpy-looking.

"Nothing. It's a little sore is all," Colette says, covering her chin with her hand. But I know better. Josianne's chin gets like that too. It happens when she's been kissing Armand and he hasn't shaved. I touch my own chin. I wonder if it'll ever look like that.

But neither Mom nor Dad seems too concerned about Colette's chin. Or that she's been spending so much time at Maxim's.

"Is Tante Hélène around when you and Maxim are hanging out?" I ask, hoping Mom and Dad will get the hint and start acting like parents again.

"Yup," Colette says, but I know she's lying. I'll bet anything that when Colette is over, Tante Hélène is busy in her kitchen making herbal potions—or brownies.

Colette runs her fingers through Mom's hair. As I watch her, I think how I haven't really touched Mom since she came home. Sure, I kiss her hello every morning, and I kiss her goodbye when I leave for work, but it's hard to hug someone who's in a wheelchair. And Mom's hair looks so greasy, I don't feel like touching it.

But Colette doesn't seem to mind. And I can see Mom's face softening. Maybe she misses us touching her.

"Let me do your hair, Mom," Colette says softly. "I'm going to make it so pretty. I'll wash it in the sink for you. It's going to smell so nice." Colette's voice is gentle, almost as if she is singing a lullaby.

Dad and I exchange looks. I think we're both worried Mom'll have another outburst.

But she doesn't. "Okay, baby," she tells Colette. "I'd like that."

Mom doesn't object when Colette wheels her into the bathroom. I follow behind, thinking Colette will probably need my help. But Colette wheels the wheelchair right over to the sink. I watch as she runs the water, testing with her fingers that it's not too hot or too cold. "Okay, you can put your head back now," she tells Mom.

Colette, who can never concentrate on anything, is concentrating now, putting a rolled up washcloth under Mom's head so she'll be more comfortable.

"Ouch!" Mom calls out suddenly. "Stop pulling my hair!"

Dad is standing behind me, and the two of us bristle at the same time. We're both expecting trouble.

Colette laughs. "Oops," she says, not bothering to apologize. "I hate it when that happens!"

The sink is full of suds. Mom sighs as Colette massages her head.

Fourteen

Dad just calls out "Bye" from the front door when he leaves to do the banking. He doesn't kiss Mom on the cheek, tug one of Colette's curls or tweak my nose. Mom doesn't seem to notice something's different, but Colette and I do.

"He didn't tweak my nose," I tell Colette once he's gone.

Colette is standing by the door, rocking on the balls of her feet. "Poor Daddy," is all she says.

Colette is working at Saintly Souvenirs today. I see her loading on the lip gloss, which means Maxim is probably going to be dropping by. I wonder if, when there are no customers, they make out there too. For a second,

I imagine Maxim's hands on Colette's grapefruit breasts and what that would feel like. But the thought disturbs me and makes my own small breasts ache in a way I'm not used to, so I make myself stop.

I'm home with Mom today. I offer to read to her, but she says no. She doesn't want to watch TV either. So I just sit with her in the living room and try to make conversation.

"Do you need a pillow for your back?"

"No."

"Do you want to see today's newspaper?"

"No."

"We could do the crossword."

"I don't think so."

"Are you hungry? I could make you a sandwich with bacon and tomato."

"Not right now."

"You sure? Because I think I'm gonna make one for myself."

"I already told you no."

On my way to the kitchen, I pause in front of Mom's wheelchair. I don't look down at her legs and feet, but I make a point of reaching out to stroke her hair. Soft and gentle, the way Colette did last night. At least now Mom's hair is clean. But her face doesn't relax the way it does when Colette touches her. Maybe Mom can sense how

117

uncomfortable I am around her. How the thought of her paralyzed legs—just hanging there, limp and useless—makes me queasy.

I wash my hands after I've laid out the bacon strips in the fry pan. Jesus is watching me from the crucifix over the sink. He's tired, aching from hanging on the cross, but even so, I can feel His disappointment. He's telling me I need to be better with Mom. More understanding, more patient, and definitely less grossed out. Mom knows exactly how I feel and so does He.

The bacon sizzles in the pan. Its smoky smell fills every corner of the kitchen and seeps into the rest of the house. When the doorbell rings, I turn down the heat.

"Don't let whoever it is in," Mom warns. "I'm not up for visitors today."

She's not up for visitors any day.

At first when I look out the glass pane on the door, I don't see anyone. Maybe it was some kid playing a trick.

But then I see a muscular suntanned arm reaching up to ring the doorbell again. The arm drops and now I see fingers in leather-and-mesh weight-lifting gloves. "Oh my God," I tell Mom. "It's him. It's Marco Leblanc."

I didn't think he ever left his house, but I can't very well leave him sitting outside our door in his rickety old wheelchair. Besides, he knows I've seen him.

Mom is wheeling herself out of the living room and into the hallway where I'm standing. "Let him in," she whispers, but I already have.

I don't like how Marco is looking at me. Staring really. As if he actually knows me.

Mom wheels herself so she is next to me. "Thérèse," Marco says. His face is all sweaty and so are his arms and hands. "It's been a while." His voice sounds rusty, which is what must happen when you hardly ever talk to anyone.

"I—uh—have to take the bacon off the stove," I say. Because I don't know what else to say, I ask Marco if he wants a bacon and tomato sandwich.

Marco looks surprised. I guess no one ever offers to make him anything. "Sure," he says. "That'd be good."

I don't really want to go back to the kitchen. Even though he gives me the creeps, I'm curious about Marco. This is the first time I've seen him up close. His upper arms are even bulkier than I thought; the blue veins near his hands are so swollen I'm afraid they might burst.

Marco has a colorful striped Mexican blanket over his lower body, but I'll bet underneath the blanket, his legs are sweating too. His hair looks like it's been dyed black. No one has hair that dark. But how could a man in a wheelchair dye his own hair? Maybe he gets the nurse to do it, or the delivery boy from the IGA.

I've got to take the bacon out of the fry pan before it burns.

"I've been watching you go up and down the ramp," I hear Marco tell Mom.

Marco speaks slowly, like it's an effort to get the words out.

"Is that so?" I don't understand why Mom isn't upset by the news that this weirdo has been stalking us.

"That's why I came. I'm worried about you."

"I thought you didn't want anything to do with me," I hear Mom say. She sounds hurt, almost as if she's disappointed Marco didn't show up on our doorstep years ago.

"I didn't. But now I do."

The bacon is draining on a paper towel, and I am slicing a ripe tomato into thin red rounds, but I don't want to miss what happens next. I lay the knife down on the counter and go to stand by the kitchen door. Marco and Mom have wheeled themselves into the living room; I can just see them from here.

Marco's wheelchair faces Mom's. But his eyes are darting around the room—up to the ceiling, over to the bed, then back up to the pair of crucifixes on the wall. It's like he's a bird that flew indoors and can't find his way out. His eyes land back on Mom. Again, I get the feeling that talking is hard for him. "You're not using your wheelchair right," he says.

When Mom laughs, it comes out sounding harsh, almost like a bark. "So you came over here to give me a lesson?"

"You got it," Marco says without lifting his eyes off her face. "If there's one thing I know something about— it's using a wheelchair. I've been in this damn thing for seventeen years." He sighs. I figure that's probably the most Marco has said to anyone in all that time.

"Seventeen years," Mom says slowly. It's as if she's remembering all the things that happened in between then and now. How she fell in love with Dad and how they had me and Colette. Maybe even how she blew smoke rings behind the Scala Santa with Emil Francoeur. "We were just teenagers. A lot happened that year."

"To all of us," Marco says softly.

"Yes, to all of us." For a minute, they're both quiet. Are they both remembering the night of Marco's accident?

Mom looks up at him. "So when are you going to show me all the things I'm doing wrong?"

Marco uses the back of his glove to wipe the sweat off his forehead. He takes a deep breath before he starts speaking again. It's not hard to see that coming over here wasn't easy for him. Maybe he's got a phobia about leaving his house. "You need to work your arms more," he tells Mom. "Most people in wheelchairs have the same problem. They use their hands. Or their feet—if their feet work. But it's a waste of energy. It's all in the arms." He flexes his arms when he says this. They're so bulky, I take a step back.

"How would you know what most people in wheelchairs do?" Mom asks, and again, I can hear that harsh laugh behind her voice. "You never leave your house."

Marco looks down at his feet, which are dangling out from under the blanket. "It's true. I don't leave the house." He sounds as if he knows there's something wrong with him. "But I watch people. And in a town like ours, a lot of people happen to be in wheelchairs."

"And now there's one more," Mom says.

Something pinches inside my chest when she says that.

"It takes strong arms to use a wheelchair right," Marco says. "All these years, with all that hiking and bicycling, you've been building up your legs—not your arms."

This guy is really creeping me out now. What's he been doing—taking notes about our family?

Mom must be thinking the same thing. "I didn't know you knew about my exercise routine."

"I'm very observant."

"Apparently," Mom says.

"Like I said, you need to use your arms more to get that chair moving right. You see this?" he asks, grabbing the round metal rim over the wheel on his wheelchair. "That's what you need to use for control. You keep getting your fingers caught in the wheel."

Mom's cheeks redden. "Now how would you know something like that?"

Marco just shrugs. "Your fingers are all messed up, aren't they?" I'm thinking the guy's probably got binoculars. How creepy is that?

"You're right," Mom says, showing Marco the tips of her fingers on her right hand. "They're all scratched up. I keep catching them in the spokes."

"That's because you're sticking your fingers in too far. You're supposed to grab just the rim." Marco wheels his wheelchair over so it's even closer to Mom's. He zips around in that thing the way Iza drives her Mini Cooper. "Like this—"

If I were Mom, I wouldn't want Marco getting so close, but she doesn't seem to mind. She doesn't seem creeped out by him the way I am.

"The occupational therapist at the hospital showed me that already," Mom tells him.

"So how come you're not doing it right?" Marco asks. I think he smiled, but it happened too fast to know for sure.

"I am."

"You're not, Thérèse." Marco looks Mom in the eye. "Don't fight me!"

"I'm not figh—" Mom stops herself in midsentence. Maybe she realizes she is fighting him—saying that stuff about how he never leaves his house and refusing to admit that she hasn't been using the wheelchair right— the way she's been fighting all of us the last couple of weeks. "Okay," Mom says, grabbing just the aluminum rim with her fingertips, "how's this?"

Marco wheels himself so close to Mom their wheel- chairs touch. When he presses his hand down on her fingers, I can't help cringing. "This is how it should feel," he tells her.

"Okay." Mom closes her eyes, as if that'll help her remember what he's showing her. "I'm getting it now."

Marco backs his wheelchair up against the bed. "Well, show me then."

Mom crosses the room in her wheelchair, then crosses back. Though she isn't half as quick as Marco, she is wheeling herself a little more smoothly and she has better control at the corners.

I know I'd better make those sandwiches before the bacon gets cold. "Would you like a glass of water with your sandwich?" I call out to Marco. He hasn't stopped sweating.

"A glass of water would be great." He looks over to where I am standing. "When you stay inside all the time, leaving's not so easy."

I pop four slices of whole-wheat bread into the toaster and take the mayonnaise from the fridge. I can still hear Mom wheeling herself around the living room. "Don't go too fast now," Marco tells her. "Especially around the corners. That's another mistake a lot of people make."

Mom's breathing hard. This is the most exercise she's had since she got home from the hospital. I think how much she used to love hiking and bicycling, how pink her cheeks got after she'd been out at the canyon, and suddenly I'm sadder than ever. Mom may never get to do those things again. It's just not right.

But Marco isn't feeling sorry for Mom the way I am. "Have you ever worked with free weights?" I hear him asking her. "I think a little weight training might help build up your biceps, triceps and shoulders. As long as you're not doing too many reps at first."

Fifteen

By the time Dad gets back, Mom is sound asleep in her wheelchair. I'm tidying up in the kitchen. "She had quite a workout this morning," I tell Dad. He's pulled a tall stool up to the kitchen counter so he can keep me company.

"A workout? What do you mean?"

"Marco came over. He gave Mom a wheelchair lesson. And he wants her to start lifting free weights."

Dad whistles. "Wow," he says, "I thought Marco never left his house. And it's been years since he talked to your mom."

I hang the fry pan on a hook over the stove. Then I turn back to Dad. "Maybe it's a miracle."

Dad tweaks my nose and we both laugh. It's a sound I haven't heard for a long time.

"I'm going to bike over to Beaupré," I tell Dad once everything is put away in the kitchen. "You okay with Mom for a bit?"

"Sure. But wear your helmet, okay? And stay on the side of the road. And look out for those eighteen-wheelers."

The wind's against me as I bike down Avenue Royale, so I have to pedal extra hard. Dad never used to worry about stuff like helmets. I guess Mom's accident is changing all of us.

There's a sporting goods store on the highway in Beaupré. In winter, they sell mostly ski equipment; in summer, bikes. I lean my bike against the metal rack outside the store. Other bikes are parked there too, and since none are locked I don't bother locking mine.

The second I open the door, I get a whiff of the dry rubbery smell of bicycle tires.

I know my way around, so I head straight for the aisle that has miscellaneous sporting equipment. I pass a stack of orange lifejackets and kayak paddles. The free weights are at the back, piled up in a pyramid. I wonder if this is where Marco got his free weights, and if so, how did he get them? Maybe one of the guys Colette and I have spotted going up to his apartment runs errands for him.

The weight-lifting gloves should be here too. I want to get Mom a pair. We've got some old free weights in the basement. This will be my way of encouraging her to use them and to build her upper body strength the way Marco says she has to.

I hear a clicking sound in the next aisle and the end of a beam of silver light flashes on the floor where I am standing. "This one's really cool," I hear someone say. The voice is familiar. But it's only when he laughs that I know for sure it's Maxim. He's checking out bicycle lights.

"Turn that thing off, will ya? It's killing my eyes." It's Armand.

I'll grab a pair of gloves for Mom—there are some pale blue ones here that look nice and are about the right size—then I'll go over and say hi to them.

But Maxim won't turn off the light. I can still see the silver beam at my feet.

"When you're out on the road at night, you gotta think about safety, man," Maxim says to Armand. "This thing's got power."

"Yeah, I can see it's got power. It's gonna blind me if you don't turn it off."

"Safety first, man, safety first. Even before your vision," Maxim says, laughing. Maxim must be pointing the beam right into Armand's eyes because I hear Armand say, "You're giving me a headache with that thing." Maxim laughs before he finally clicks the light off.

"If you cared so much about safety"—Armand drops his voice a little so I have to lean into the glove display to hear him—"you'd have used a condom with your girl-friend the other night."

The tops of my ears feel like they're on fire. If Maxim had used a condom the other night! Armand had better be talking about some old girlfriend Maxim's got in Quebec City! Colette's impulsive, but she'd never have unprotected sex. Or would she? Besides, Colette's my little sister. She can't be having sex before me!

No, there's no way she'd have unprotected sex. Not after all the warnings we get in MRE. Even Mom and Dad have talked to us about safe sex. It wasn't easy for Mom because she's so religious—I've never seen her blush like that—but Dad said we needed to be well-informed, that it was a matter of our personal safety.

When Maxim speaks, he doesn't even bother to lower his voice. It's as if he doesn't care if the whole world hears him trashtalking. "Yeah, Colette wanted me to use one, but I talked her out of it. And she was too excited to argue...if you know what I mean." He practically hoots when he says this. "Man, that girl's wild!"

My first thought is, there's no way Maxim can be talking about my sister. Maybe his old girlfriend's name was Colette too.

The pale blue weight-lifting gloves have fallen out of my hands and are lying on the floor.

"I sure wish Josianne would let me do it without a condom," Armand says.

Sixteen

I nearly say something right then and there to Maxim. I nearly go over, tap him on the shoulder and tell him what an irresponsible jerk he is and how, even if he can fool everyone else in Ste-Anne-de-Beaupré, including his grandmother, he can't fool me! That I can see right through his smarmy act!

But in the end, I decide Maxim isn't the person I need to talk to—Colette is. So I wait for Maxim and Armand to leave the store. Besides, it takes a while for my heart to stop racing.

Maxim doesn't buy the light. I guess he's not as concerned about safety as he says!

My hands shake as I pay for the pale blue weight-lifting gloves. I'm a little afraid that every time I see them I'm going to remember the disgusting conversation I just overheard. *Man, that girl's wild!*

Biking helps calm me down. As I pedal, I plan what I'll say to Colette. She can't keep having sex without a condom. And who knows? It may already be too late! What if she's pregnant—or Maxim has given her an STD? Judging from the way he talked, he's been with other girls, besides Colette.

The road into town is busier than usual. It's already the beginning of July and Ste-Anne-de-Beaupré is getting more crowded every day. Still, it's nothing compared to how busy it's going to be on July 25, Saint Anne's feast day.

When I burst through the door at Saintly Souvenirs, I see there are customers in the store. Two women, wearing matching pink sweater sets and carrying the same pale pink purses. Maybe it's a good thing Colette isn't alone—otherwise, I might strangle her.

"I want twenty vials of your miracle oil," one of the women tells Colette. The other one is looking at post-cards of the basilica. They both have fine reddish hair and freckled arms. Sisters, probably, or two women who've been friends so long they've started to look alike.

"Coming right up," Colette says, smiling. Somehow, I expect Colette to look different. More grown up. Sinful. Like a person who's had sex. Unprotected sex. But Colette looks the same as always. Bright-eyed, with those big brown curls that make you want to touch them. Maxim must've touched them. He must've touched a lot more too, and not just her breasts. The thought makes the insides of my thighs tingle and I cross my legs to make the tingling stop. How could Colette have let him? How could she have been so...so...irresponsible?

"You never know when you're going to need a miracle," the first woman says as Colette counts out the vials and wraps them in tissue paper. The other woman chooses a postcard of the Miraculous Statue and brings it to the cash.

"Are you two twins?" Colette asks the women. That's when she spots me—and waves. "Hey, Ani!"

"We're sisters, not twins, but every bit as close as twins. Aren't we, Cheryl?" the postcard sister says, squeezing the other one's fat freckly arm.

"No one understands you better than a sister," Cheryl says, and then the two of them turn and grin at each other like they've just won the mini-lotto. I'll bet neither of them ever had unprotected sex. Or any kind of sex at all.

"That's my sister," Colette says, and the two women turn around and peer at me as if I'm a rare zoo animal.

"You two don't look anything alike," the postcard sister says.

"Not a bit," Cheryl agrees. Then she taps her chest as if to show us it's not hollow. "Of course, it's not the looks that matter. It's the heart connection."

"Well, we've got that for sure," Colette says, grinning up at me.

Yeah, I'm thinking, if wanting to murder your sister counts as a heart connection.

The two women take forever to leave the store. Cheryl is cleaning out her purse, emptying its contents on the counter. Her wallet, a lipstick, a pair of reading glasses with rhinestone decorations. "I know I have a dollar in here somewhere," she says. The postcard sister wonders out loud whether she should have chosen a different postcard.

"I need to talk to you," I tell Colette. "It's important."

"What's up?" she asks.

"I can't talk until they leave," I whisper.

"I hope you get your miracles!" Colette calls out when the sisters finally take off.

"Lovely to have met the two of you!" the sisters say in chorus. Even their matching pale pink purses swing on their shoulders in unison as they head out to the sidewalk.

"Is Mom okay?" Colette asks. She's bouncing, but she has one hand on the counter, steadying her.

"Mom's okay. I came to talk about you. And Maxim." I even hate saying that creep's name. "I was at the sporting goods store in Beaupré. He was there too. I heard him talking to Armand. About you."

Colette's face brightens. "What did he say? Did he call me his girlfriend? Did he say he thinks I'm beautiful? Well, did he?"

Though I know we're alone, I turn around to make sure no one is listening. I'm embarrassed even to say what I'm about to say around the Jesus statues and the crucifixes. Someone in this town needs to be discreet. I take a deep breath. "He said the two of you had"—I gulp a little—"sex without a condom. Is that true, Colette?" I don't care if I sound angry and judgmental. I am angry—and I am judging Colette.

"I don't want to talk about it." Colette's lower lip trembles. Now I know what Maxim said has to be true.

"Colette! What in God's name were you were thinking? You're too young to have sex! And you know how dangerous unprotected sex is! You could have a terrible disease, AIDS even! And you could be pregnant!

Don't you know anyth—?" I only stop shouting when my voice breaks.

I expect Colette to start bawling. If I were her, I'd feel guilty and lost and scared to death. I'd feel like I'd ruined my whole life. But when Colette looks up at me, her eyes are dry. "It was awesome!" she says.

At first, I'm not sure I've heard her right. "Awesome?" I step so close to Colette I can hear her breathing. "Are you nuts?"

She's breathing faster now. "Well, maybe the first time wasn't awesome. The first time hurt a little." I can't believe Colette is telling me this. Can't she see how she's embarrassing me? Even my neck feels hot. But Colette doesn't notice. "After that first time, it was awesome. Definitely awesome. And fun." Now she's looking right at me, reminding me that though I'm the older sister, when it comes to sex, she knows way more than I do.

I feel my jaw drop open, but no words come out. I'm too upset to speak.

Colette sighs as if I'm the one who's done something stupid. "What would you know about fun, Ani? You're the least fun person I ever met. And you're jealous too! That's why you're yelling at me. You're just plain jealous!"

"Jealous?" Now she's really making me angry. Why doesn't she understand I'm looking out for her—the way

I always do? The way I've had to ever since she was born! "What do I have to be jealous about?" I'm shrieking now. "That you have some loser boyfriend who can't keep his mouth shut? And who doesn't respect you enough to use a condom?"

When I slap Colette, it feels like my hand is moving without me. As if it slipped out from under my sleeve to smack her cheek. As if the red mark on her cheek appeared out of nowhere and had nothing to do with me.

It's not fair that I'm the one who ends up crying. Colette's been irresponsible, not me. I'm just trying to protect her. Only I can't protect her anymore. That's the problem.

I can't go home. Not feeling like this. There's no way I can tell Mom and Dad about Colette. They've already got too much to worry about. Besides, if Mom and Dad found out, they'd go to war. Dad would focus on Colette's safety; Mom would pray for Colette's soul.

I'm afraid if I get back on my bike, I'll fall off. So I end up walking alongside my bike, trying to calm down. The hand I used to slap Colette feels hot. I don't care if I left a mark on her cheek. I don't care if it never goes away. Colette deserves it—for being such an idiot. For falling for a loser like Maxim. For having sex with him. A guy who flirts with middle-aged waitresses.

I take one of the smaller roads off Avenue Royale. I don't want to run into anyone I know. I need to gather my thoughts. Make a plan. This is the sort of problem a mom's supposed to handle, not a sister.

Colette will have to have a pregnancy test. And an HIV/AIDS test too. Who knows how many other girls Maxim has sweet-talked into unprotected sex? When Colette calms down, I'll tell her she needs to ask him. And that if she plans to keep having sex with him, they'll have to use a condom.

My head is hurting from trying to sort all this out.

Maybe that's why I don't see Tante Hélène coming up the sidewalk toward me. I smell dandelions before I see her. She's carrying a bundle of the bright yellow weeds.

"Ani?" she says, stopping in front of me. "What's wrong?" She puts her dandelions in my bicycle basket and slides the palm of her hand against my forehead. "You have a fever. Not high, but a fever nonetheless. You should sit down. Come, dear, we're not far from my house."

I feel my legs wobble as we follow the sidewalk to her house. I leave my bike on her lawn. Tante Hélène leads me to the chipped blue swing on her front porch and sits me down on the puffy pillow. It feels damp under my bum.

"How about a nice cup of dandelion tea?"

I can't even stand the smell of dandelions. "No thanks. I'll just sit for a bit."

Tante Hélène is watching my face. "You're not really sick, are you?" she says. "You're upset. I can tell. The dandelion tea would do you good."

"Okay, I'll have some." There's no use fighting Tante Hélène.

Maybe it's because she's added honey, but the dandelion tea doesn't taste bitter. And if I don't inhale when I drink it, I don't notice the bad smell. I am beginning to feel a little calmer. Maybe it's the tea, or maybe it's from sitting next to Tante Hélène on her porch swing. The swing is rocking just a little, kind of like a cradle.

"This business with your mother must be very hard on all of you," Tante Hélène says with a sigh and I nod. "But that's not all that's bothering you, is it?"

How does she know stuff like that?

"It's my sister," I say into my teacup. "And your grandson." At least I don't have to say his name.

"My grandson?" Tante Hélène seems surprised that anything about her grandson could be a problem. He's got her under his spell too. "I know he and Colette have been spending a great deal of time together," she says. She makes it sound as if they've been playing checkers up in his bedroom. "They seem to have become very close friends."

"They're more than close friends," I whisper.

Tante Hélène nods. "It's the way of the world," she says. "There's no stopping it. There never was."

"Maxim and Colette...you know..." I feel my ears getting hot again. I can't believe I'm saying these things—or trying to—to Maxim's grandmother. I take another sip of dandelion tea. "They did it...without...you know..."

When Tante Hélène bites her lip, I know she understands what I'm trying to tell her. "Oh my," she says. "Oh my. That's very bad. Very worrisome."

At least now I'm not the only one worrying. The thought makes me feel just a little bit better.

"I'll talk to him. Straightaway." Tante Hélène's chin wobbles when she says so.

"You will? You'd talk to him about...well, you know...?"

"Of course I know. In fact, I should have talked to him when he first came to stay with me. And I'll talk to Colette too."

"You will?"

"Certainly. Colette and I have become good friends."

"You have?" I try to picture Colette sitting here, sipping dandelion tea and chatting with Tante Hélène. I've seen Colette on swings. If Colette was on this one, she'd rock so hard, she'd send Tante Hélène flying all the way to Avenue Royale.

"She'll need to go to the clinic. For a checkup. I have an old friend who works there. I'll phone and see what she can do."

"Do you think Colette could be—?" I bite my lip.

Tante Hélène brushes some strands of gray hair away from her eyes. "Let's hope not."

We both sip at our tea. I can feel Tante Hélène's eyes on my face. I get the feeling she's about to prescribe some herbal remedy for me. Something to bring down my fever, settle my stomach or calm my nerves.

But that's not what Tante Hélène has on her mind.

"You seem a little squeamish," she says. "About sex." Tante Hélène says the word like it's no big deal. As if there's nothing sinful about it.

First I look down at my feet. Then I look over at my bicycle lying on the lawn. I don't know where to look next. "I don't like talking about it is all. It's…embarrassing."

For a moment, Tante Hélène closes her eyes. Her eyelids look like they're made of tissue paper. "In my day," she says, "we never discussed sex. How I wish I'd had someone to talk to about such things when I was a young woman. All the new feelings in my body. Feelings that sometimes made me feel ashamed."

Listening to her makes me remember the feelings I've been having lately. New feelings. The tingling I got in church when Father Francoeur looked at me, the ache in my breasts when I imagined Maxim touching Colette.

Tante Hélène continues. "It wasn't that much better when your mother was growing up either. Especially for Catholic girls."

Though Tante Hélène is old and wrinkled, I don't find it that hard to imagine her as a teenager. I wonder what she thought about sex when she was a teenager. "How did you find stuff out—in your day, I mean?"

When Tante Hélène chuckles, her cheeks fill up and she reminds me of a squirrel. "Well, mostly through trial and error. But birth control—oh my, we knew nothing about it. Not a thing! The priests told us birth control was a sin. They told us sex was just for having babies. It's no wonder people had so many children in those days. Too many! The women were just plain worn out from raising such big families. No one told us sex could be pleasurable."

Pleasurable. Tante Hélène smiles when she says it.

I think about what Colette had said about fun. About how I was the least fun person she'd ever met. What if that's true? "I don't even like to think about sex. I mean... I do think about it, quite a lot sometimes, but I try not to." The words have slipped out of me, and immediately I'm sorry I said them. I've told Tante Hélène too much. She'll think I'm as bad as Colette.

But Tante Hélène only pats my hair and sighs. "One day, when you care for somebody, and when your body's ready, you won't mind thinking about it," she says. "You probably won't be able to stop thinking about it! And one day, when you're an old woman like me, you'll be able to explain things to a young woman like you. And that way, we make things a little better. For all of us."

The two of us rock for a while on the swing. I lift my feet as the swing rises. One of my sandals falls off. I let the other one fall off too. The summer air tickles the skin between my toes.

"So you'll talk to Maxim and Colette—and you'll call your friend at the clinic?" I ask Tante Hélène before I go.

"Of course I will. You know, Ani"—for a moment Tante Hélène's eyes sparkle—"you aren't the only take-charge person in this town."

Seventeen

Did all the peonies just burst into bloom in the last half hour?

Because I hadn't noticed them before—not on my bike ride to Beaupré, and not on the way back into town. Now I see them everywhere. Pink ones, white ones, fuchsia ones so dark they're almost black. It's as if they've all opened at the same time. The blooms are already heavy and lush-looking, drooping from their stems. When I get off my bike at the top of our street, I catch a whiff of peony that reminds me of all my summers in Ste-Anne-de-Beaupré. I bend down to admire the soft pink petals. Tante Hélène was right when she said nature is a miracle.

I'm careful not to let my nose touch the flower. Peonies are full of ants. I know because Mom used to hold them upside down and shake them out like a mop after she picked them. Colette would scour the grass afterward, trying to find the ants so she could return them to their anthill in the flowerbed.

"They'll find a new anthill," Mom would tell her.

Colette would shake her head. "No, they'll want to go home. To their own anthill."

Oh my. Father Francoeur is across the street. I see him on Marco Leblanc's balcony, and now I see his Toyota parked on the street. I remember how Father Francoeur told me he'd drop by sometime to see Marco. That they're old friends, though that's still hard to imagine.

I try not to stare. But I do notice Father Francoeur is wearing his priest's collar. He's on Marco's balcony, squatting in front of Marco's wheelchair, his hands on Marco's giant forearms. The two of them are talking. I wonder about what. Old times? Father Francoeur's work at the Liberian leper colony? Weight lifting?

I straighten my shoulders and flip my hair so it hangs long and straight against my back. I know my hair is my best feature. Too bad I'm not wearing Colette's lip gloss. I lick my lips to make them shiny. And I take my time walking up to our front door. There, they've seen me!

Marco nods (which is a lot for him). Father Francoeur lifts his hand and smiles. It's a small wave and a small smile, but still my heart beats a little faster.

Father Francoeur still has one hand on Marco's forearm. "God be with you," I hear him tell Marco. Then he puts his arms around Marco and hugs him. Hard. I guess there is a way of hugging someone in a wheelchair. I wonder if I should try it on Mom.

The old green plastic watering can is out on our front steps. Dad must've filled it with water a few days ago, because there's a thin layer of oily black scum at the top. I figure the flowers won't mind a bit of scum, so I take the can—it's heavier than I expect—and start watering the pots of geraniums by our door. Mom and Dad planted them on Victoria Day weekend. Before things went crazy.

Please, Dad, don't pop out of the house and ask why I've taken a sudden interest in plants. How could I tell Dad I'm hoping to talk to a priest? About religion, of course.

When Father Francoeur comes down Marco's staircase, he's wiping his cheek. Was he crying? After Mom's accident, Dad got angry but he didn't cry. Except for in movies or on TV, I don't think I've ever seen a man cry, so I don't know what to do. Am I supposed to turn away to give Father Francoeur privacy—or do I say something kind? It's hard to know and I don't have much time to decide. But I want to do the right thing. I want to be there for Father Francoeur. The way he was there for me after Mom's accident.

In the end, it's Father Francoeur who comes over and speaks to me. I've stretched my arm way out to water one of the hanging pots. Father Francoeur touches the back of my shoulder and I get that tingle again, the kind I get after my foot falls asleep, only better, and now the tingle is in my shoulder exactly where he touched me. For a moment, I'm afraid I'll spill the water that's left in the can on Father Francoeur's shiny loafers. "How are things, Ani?" he asks. His voice is even gentler than I remember.

"They're okay, I guess. So you went to see Marco—like you said you would." I want Father Francoeur to know I admire him for keeping his promises. Lots of people don't.

Father Francoeur nods. "It's been a long time," he says. "Too long. Marco and I had a lot to tell each other."

Father Francoeur must be able to tell I'm surprised. "Marco and I used to be pretty tight," he says. Then Father Francoeur looks right at me, and it takes all my courage not to look away. "I was with Marco the night he got hit by the train."

I don't say anything at first. I'm picturing the accident, Marco's body trapped under the train. I'm imagining the sound of Marco's scream. Did he see the train coming?

"I never knew," I say. "About who was with him, I mean. Only that Marco was drunk. Were you drunk too?" It's a Colette-type question. But if Mom and Father Francoeur smoked behind the Scala Santa, maybe Father Francoeur also used to drink.

"No, not really. Marco drank too much in those days. Drinking helped him forget." Father Francoeur takes a deep breath. "But I shouldn't have let him go home alone that night. He shouldn't have been anywhere near the tracks. Not in the condition he was in." Father Francoeur sighs.

For a moment, I get this strange dizzy feeling, the kind of feeling I used to get when I was little and I spun myself round and round, and suddenly stopped. How odd is it that a priest is confessing to me? Because that's what this feels like. As if Father Francoeur is confessing and he wants me to absolve him. Except that he can see my face and there isn't a mesh window separating us the way there is in a confession booth. And I'm not a priest.

Father Francoeur shakes his head. "I haven't thought about that night for a long time, Ani. It changed Marco's life. And mine too." Father Francoeur tilts his neck back and looks up at the sky.

I know he's talking about his decision to become a priest. And I know, too, that Father Francoeur is sharing something important with me. Something he thinks

I'll understand. I can practically feel my heart opening in my chest. Like one of those peonies.

Leave it to Colette to ruin the moment. She comes bouncing up Avenue Royale just then. I hope she won't say anything about our latest fight. I don't want Father Francoeur to think I'm mean. But Colette is smiling and though her cheek is still a little red, you can't really tell I slapped her.

Colette doesn't bear grudges. Maybe it's part of her ADHD but she can't seem to concentrate long enough to stay upset with someone. It's kind of nice.

"Hey, Father Francoeur," Colette says. Her head is going up and down like one of those bobblehead dolls we used to collect. "What's up?"

I can't believe Colette just said "What's up?" to a priest. But Father Francoeur doesn't seem to mind. He smiles at Colette like she's a frisky puppy, like she's another miracle. I wonder what he'd say if he knew about her and Maxim. I'll bet he wouldn't smile so much. "Did you come to see Mom?" Colette asks him.

"Actually, I came to see Marco. And I've just had a good chat with your big sister here." Again, Father Francoeur touches my shoulder. Even when he takes his hand away, I still feel his touch. Then Father Francoeur checks his watch. I notice the fine brown hairs on his wrist.

"It looks like I'll need to come back another time to visit your mom. I'm due at the Blessings Office. Last week, a woman wanted me to bless her new toaster. And someone else wanted me to bless their canary." That makes Colette and me both laugh. "But tell your mom I'm praying for her. For all of you. Every day."

I watch Father Francoeur as he walks down the wheel-chair ramp. Before he gets into his car, Father Francoeur looks up at Marco Leblanc's balcony. But Marco's not there; he must have wheeled himself inside while I was talking to Father Francoeur.

"You know you could be a little less obvious about it," Colette says.

"About what?" I'm still watching the back of Father Francoeur's head as he drives off.

"About your crush on him."

"What crush?"

"Your crush on Father Francoeur."

"I don't have a crush on him!" I say quickly. "We've just got a…a"—I'm looking for the right word—"a connection."

"A crush is a crush," Colette says. "But you hafta admit, Ani, it is pretty gross." She wrinkles up her nose. "I mean, the guy's old enough to be your father."

Eighteen

I hear a car door slam. Who's out at this hour? Another insomniac, I guess.

Tante Hélène says chamomile tea helps when you can't sleep. Only we don't have any in the house. Colette is sound asleep. Sometimes I think I do all her worrying for her.

Colette had a fit when I told her I'd talked to Tante Hélène. Her eyes narrowed, just like Eeyore's do when he's mad. "I'm never going to speak to you again. Ever."

The silent treatment didn't last long. I knew it wouldn't. Not coming from someone who likes talking as much as Colette does.

She wouldn't look at me for fifteen minutes, which made me feel awful. But then she punched my arm and told me, "I know you meant well. But sometimes you can be a bit of an idiot."

"Look who's talking!" I said, and that was pretty much the end of that argument.

Tante Hélène got Colette an appointment at the clinic. She also talked to her and Maxim about safe sex. "She's pretty cool—for an old lady," Colette told me, "so you can stop worrying now."

But worrying isn't some switch I can just turn off.

And it's worse at night when the only light comes from the green glow of the numbers on our clock radio.

Even though it's 2:00 AM (I know because I just checked), Mom and Dad are talking in the living room, where their bed is set up. All I can hear are whispers, then silence, then more whispers. Dad is doing more talking than Mom, and the rhythm of their conversation—what sounds like a question, then a long pause, then another more urgent question—makes me think they're talking about something important.

When Colette and I were little, and Mom and Dad had Iza's parents over, Colette and I used to sit at the bottom of the back stairs and listen in to the adults' conversation. It was Colette's idea. If Iza's dad made a joke, I'd give

Colette a stern look so she'd know not to laugh and give us away. Colette would cover her mouth to hold the laugh in. I don't think Mom and Dad ever knew about our hiding spot.

Because I'm wondering what's so important that Mom and Dad have to talk about it now, I slip out of our room and down the hallway to the back stairway. I stop on the fifth stair from the bottom—our old listening place. When I sit down, the wood feels worn under my nightgown. The stairway is so narrow it's hard to imagine Colette and me ever fitting together on one step.

"I never asked you before," I can hear Dad saying. His voice sounds sad and tense and worn out all at the same time.

"I've always appreciated that," Mom tells him. "You always said it didn't matter. Why should it matter now—after so long?"

"I'm not sure, Thérèse. It just does."

Neither of them says anything now, and I stay in my spot, trying not to move a muscle. I have no idea what "it" is. I figured they'd be talking about Mom's condition, but "it" seems to be something else altogether. Something that happened long ago and that's got nothing to do with Mom's accident.

"This is hard for me too, Thérèse," I hear Dad say.

Mom makes a snorting sound. "Am I supposed to feel sorry for you now? Because you're married to a cripple." Mom sounds more angry than sad.

"You're not a cripple. You're you. You've always been you. The you I fell in love with."

Now I hear their bed creak—then nothing for a long time. Dad's voice breaks the silence. "Would you like another pillow for under your legs, Thérèse?"

"I'm fine like this."

Dad sighs. It's pretty obvious Mom's not going to tell him whatever it is he wants to know.

It feels like I'll never fall asleep again. Like I'll spend the rest of my nights sitting on this staircase. Being inside isn't helping. Maybe it's the narrow staircase, but the walls feel like they're pressing in on me.

Except for when Mom used to hang out the laundry, we hardly ever use the back door at the bottom of this stairway. Because I'm wearing my fuzzy pink slippers, I reach the landing without making any noise. When I unlatch the door, I hang on to the brass chain so it won't rattle. The night air feels warm and soft, and the crickets are singing to each other. When I look up at the sky and see the full moon hovering over the cliff, I feel a little less lonely.

The wrought-iron table and chairs are out here, but because I don't feel like sitting, I walk round the house to the front. Eeyore is in the kitchen window. Is it my imagination or does he wink at me?

I feel Marco Leblanc before I see him. He's on his balcony. I look over at his shadowy figure, hunched in his wheelchair…and then I realize he's not alone. There is someone else on the balcony with him. The person is sitting on a plastic lawn chair across from Marco. And I'm pretty sure the person is stroking Marco's face.

I know disabled people have lives, but somehow, the possibility of Marco having relationships with anyone besides the nurse from the clinic and the delivery guy from the IGA never occurred to me. I thought the guys who came to visit were his friends. I never pictured him being somebody's boyfriend. I wonder what the two of them talk about. I mean, until recently, I didn't know he could talk.

They haven't noticed me. I like the feeling of being able to watch Marco—it's a way of getting even for all the times he watched us without our knowing it.

Now I notice something else—leaning against the side of the balcony where Marco keeps his weights. At first I think it's another person, but then I realize it's a guitar case. Maybe Marco's girlfriend is a musician.

It's only when the girlfriend leans over to take the guitar out of the case that I realize the girlfriend isn't a girl. Girls don't have such broad shoulders and wide backs.

It's a boyfriend. Marco's gay.

Why didn't I figure it out before? It explains the different men Colette and I have spotted over the years going up to Marco's apartment. It even explains his bulked-up chest and dyed hair. I wonder if Colette already knows. And though I'd rather not think about it, I wonder about the kinds of sex stuff Marco and his boyfriend do to each other.

I need to get out of here, go for a long walk, clear my head, only now I'm really trapped. More trapped even than when I was lying in my bed, sleepless, or sitting on the stairs, eavesdropping on Mom and Dad. If I move now, Marco will know I've been spying on him. On them.

The boyfriend is strumming the guitar. Each chord seems to hover in the air as if the sounds know how to float. "*When I find myself in times of trouble, Mother Mary comes to me...*" I have to admit the boyfriend has a good voice—gravelly and gentle both. He's singing an old Beatles song—I know because it's one of Mom's favorites. "*Let it be, let it be...*"

Even the crickets have stopped chirping so they can listen.

I wonder how many nights Marco's boyfriend has come to sing to him. I guess I've been wrong about Marco. He has a life.

The song is calming me down. It's chamomile tea set to music.

Marco applauds when the song is over, and the boyfriend gets up and takes a low bow.

"I'd better get going," I hear him tell Marco. "I've got to be on the road early tomorrow. But I'll see you next week when I'm back. On Wednesday."

"You drive safe," I hear Marco say. "Call me from the road. If you can."

"Don't I always call from the road?"

Marco laughs.

I try not to stare when the two of them kiss. On the lips and for a really long time. It's not as if I've never heard about gay people, but I've never seen them—you know—in action. What would Father Francoeur say? And do Mom and Dad know Marco's gay? Have they known all along?

The boyfriend packs up his guitar, slings the case over his shoulder and heads down the exterior staircase and into a car parked outside. Marco has wheeled himself over to the edge of his balcony. He watches the car's red taillights as they disappear into the night.

"Can't sleep?"

Marco's question catches me by surprise. How long has he known I was out here—watching him?

"Yeah. I share a room with Colette. She's sound asleep." I don't know why I'm telling him all this. Probably because I'm nervous.

"Nighttime's good for thinking."

It's as if I can still hear the song lyrics drifting in the night air. *Let it be. Let it be.* How nice it must be to be able to do that—let things be. But I'm not much good at doing that.

"I worry more at night," I tell Marco.

"Most people do. You worrying about your mom?"

"Yeah, my mom. And about us too. Sometimes I think our family's falling apart."

Marco nods but doesn't say anything. I'm glad he's not offering advice the way most adults do if you say you're upset.

"My parents aren't getting along so well," I tell him. It's an understatement.

Marco looks across the street at our house as if he can see inside. "Your parents have worked a lot of things out. They'll work this one out too."

"You sure?" I don't know why his opinion suddenly matters so much.

Marco nods again. "I'm sure."

"So I guess that guy was your boyfriend, right?" He must know I saw them kissing.

"Right." Marco doesn't sound embarrassed. That makes me feel less embarrassed too.

"Have you two been together a long time?"

"I didn't know you were so curious. I thought your sister was the curious one."

Maybe Marco doesn't want to talk about his boyfriend. For a bit, neither of us says anything. But the silence between us isn't an uncomfortable one.

"Wanna come up and have a seat?"

"I guess."

I've never been up on Marco's balcony. I climb the stairs and, even in the dark, I can tell everything has a spot. The weights are piled in their corner; there's a tray for food and a pile of neatly stacked newspapers.

I sit in the chair where Marco's boyfriend sat. The seat is still warm. For a second, I smell the boyfriend's lemony aftershave, and then the smell is gone.

When I adjust my feet, I knock something over under the chair. It's an empty beer can, and now I can feel there's another one under the chair too. "I thought you didn't drink."

"I don't. But Jean-Pierre likes a beer or two when he comes by. He's got a job driving one of those eighteen-wheelers, so he's out on the road all day. I used to drink too much." For a second, it feels like Marco is talking to the night, not to me. "That's how I got into the accident. The one that left me this way." He waves one hand over his legs.

"I know. Father Francoeur told me. He said he was with you the night it happened."

Marco winces. I wonder what he remembers from the accident. Did he see the train coming down the tracks? "What else did Father Francoeur tell you?"

"That you guys used to hang out. And that my mom taught him how to smoke."

"Yeah, Emil and your mom were pretty tight in those days."

"Why'd you drink so much back then?"

"Let me guess," Marco says. "You've never been drunk." When he smiles, his face looks a little lopsided.

"Of course not. I'm under eighteen." As soon as I say it, I realize how dumb I must sound. Lots of kids drink before it's legal. Marco did. "You still didn't say why you used to drink so much."

The crickets are singing again. Were they singing the night of his accident too?

"Maybe I was trying to run away." Marco waves at his legs again. I know what he's telling me: now he can never run away. In all the years Marco has been our neighbor, this is the first time I've ever imagined what it must feel like to be him. He's more trapped than me.

"What were you running away from?" I'm expecting Marco to say the cliff and the highway and the basilica, but that isn't what he tells me.

"I was running away from me." Marco pauses. I know he's remembering again. "From knowing I was gay. From thinking it was a sin. But you can't run away from who you are. Even if your legs work right."

Nineteen

I wake up too tired to stretch, too tired even to turn onto my other side. Is this what being paraplegic feels like? I bend one knee, just because I can.

I feel as if I've been awake all night. I had the weirdest dreams. I can't recall details, only the terrible feeling that I've been very, very bad.

Slowly, as I lie curled on my side, pieces of my dreams start coming back. At first, it's just images: a checker-board; a dish of ripe mango slices; my hand sweeping statues off a shelf at Saintly Souvenirs; a mouth, wide-open and hungry-looking. There's a soundtrack too. The statues clattering to the ground; a crash of thunder;

someone moaning. I try to push the memories away, but the images and sounds won't go.

What were the matchy-match sisters doing in my dreams? They were outside Saintly Souvenirs, peering at the window display. Only the display was all wrong. The huge Jesus on the cross was laughing, and instead of the tiny Jesuses inside the snow globes, there were miniature me's. And the miniature me's were wearing hot pink short shorts and a bikini top.

"I need a few more vials of miracle oil," one matchy-match sister said to the other.

In my dream, I tapped on her shoulder. So hard she stumbled. "You're wasting your money. There's no such thing as miracles," I said.

She looked as if I'd slapped her. Remembering this makes me feel terrible. But in my dream, it was different. I was different. I didn't care about that silly woman's feelings. Imagine two old ladies dressed in matching clothes!

There was more. Now I see my dream self marching into Saintly Souvenirs. Colette was at the counter, setting up our old cardboard checkerboard. "You go first," she said, smiling up at me. But instead of taking a turn, I hit the board with the side of my hand and sent the red and black discs flying.

Now I remember a smell. The sweet, heavy smell of ripe mangoes. Colette was laying the bright orange slices on a tray. "No, no," she said, pushing me away when I reached for one, "they're not for you, Ani. You're allergic, remember?"

But I grabbed a fistful of mango slices and shoved them into my mouth. Their sticky juice dribbled down my chin, then down my neck. In my dream, I didn't bother wiping it away.

"Oh no!" Colette said, covering her mouth.

But in the dream, I didn't go into anaphylactic shock the way I would if I ate mango in real life. In the dream, there was hot black lava churning inside me; I was a volcano about to explode. "What do you know?" I shouted at Colette. "You're a stupid slut!"

Colette's eyes were all pupil.

I can't believe I called her a slut, even if it was a dream. Me—Saint Ani! But in the dream, I felt good. Free. Strong. As if I'd climbed to the top of Mount Everest and shouted at the top of my lungs. As if nothing could hold me back. Not having to be kind or responsible. Not having to be anything like my saintly namesake.

And now I see another piece of my dream. A shorter one. I was leaving the shop. As I left, I ran the side of my hand along the shelf of miniature porcelain statues of Jesus and Saint Anne.

The statues tumbled to the ground. I knew from the clattering sounds some were broken. There would be shards of porcelain on the floor. But I didn't care. Let Colette vacuum up the mess.

I was tired of cleaning up after her.

I cover my eyes with my hands. What does it mean if the me in my dreams is so cold and cruel and angry? Can all those feelings be inside me too?

Oh no, there's more. Maxim was in my dreams too! He was walking into Sweet Heaven.

I marched right up to him. I wasn't going to skulk around the way I did in the sporting goods store. Skulking wasn't my style. Not in last night's dreams, anyhow! Maxim shoved his hands into his pockets. "What's up?" he said, all Mr. Cool. "You look really good, today, Ani— like you're on fire."

I was on fire!

"You're full of shit," I told him.

His mouth fell open. Then he laughed. A big laugh that made his face twist up. "I can't believe you said that. Colette says you never swear."

This time I laughed. "I do now!" Then I stepped a little closer to him and I was glad when he stepped back. "Maybe Colette and other people fall for your bullshit, but I don't. I know exactly what kind of"—I stopped to choose my words—"selfish, phony asshole you are."

I can't believe I said those things. I don't think I ever even thought them before.

Do other people say and do terrible things in their dreams? Or is it just me?

Maxim has vanished, and now more fragments are coming back. I want to make it stop, but I can't. My mind wants me to remember—wants me to know how bad I really am.

I was on Avenue Royale. I was a giant and my legs were stilts. When I passed Saintly Souvenirs, the store seemed suddenly tiny and very far away, like I was seeing it through the wrong end of a telescope.

In the next snippet of dream, I was walking under the center arch of the basilica. I had a plan: I was going to make the walls and golden ceiling shake. I was going to make the statues cover their mouths and groan. Whoever said churches had to be quiet? Quiet and rules were for the old Ani; the dream Ani wanted noise and chaos.

I'm still curled up on my side, trying to make sense of all the pieces, when my body does something weird: it shudders. The shudder shoots down my spine like electricity, then spreads around my belly and between my thighs. The feeling was in my dreams too.

Someone's hand was on my waist. It was a soft warm hand and it was reaching under my nightgown, grazing the tops of my breasts, moving over my belly and toward the band of skin just above the top of my underwear. I didn't know who was touching me like that—and I didn't care. All I knew was I didn't want the feeling to stop. No one had ever touched me that way, made my skin feel like every inch of it was alive.

"Ani, you look like you're on fire."

Maxim's mouth was open, and his teeth were very white, but he wasn't laughing. I could hear a faint moaning sound in the distance.

Maxim was touching my waist, his fingers making small round flutters.

My thighs were hot and strangely heavy. I really was on fire.

"Kiss me," I said, reaching up for the back of his head.

I remember what I was thinking: So this is what it feels like to want someone. It's why Colette said yes even when Maxim didn't want to use a condom.

The dream me ran my fingers through his hair. It was so thick and soft and dark. I can still see it, feel it even.

But that doesn't make sense. Maxim's hair's not dark.

A wave of shame so big I'm sure I'll drown washes over me.

And now I realize it's my own hand under my night-gown, moving down my belly. I'm aching again. And that moaning sound is coming from me. I pull my hand out from under my nightgown and shake my head. I have to make the dreams—and the achy feeling—go away.

The pillow is damp near where my mouth is. My thighs still feel hot and heavy.

I might have been dreaming, but I know one thing for sure: the feelings—all of them—were real.

Outside, the bottom of the sky is beginning to turn pink. I pull the pillow out from behind me and throw it over my head. I need to sleep some more. Just sleep—not dream.

Twenty

The basilica museum is smaller than I remember. Why does that always happen when I go back to a place I haven't been in a long time?

The museum doesn't have many sculptures or old paintings the way other museums do. There's an ancient wheelchair with wooden wheels, though I doubt it's worth much, even on eBay.

Colette, Iza and Josianne are with me. The lady at the information desk perks up when she sees us. "It's wonderful to see young people take an interest in our collection. You girls give me hope for the future of the church."

"We're not really interested in religion," Colette tells the lady. "We're here for Father Francoeur's lecture.

My friend," she says, turning to Iza, "thinks she'd like to do community work in Africa some day. And my sister—"

That's when I tug on Colette's arm and drag her toward the all-purpose room where the lecture is going to be. Along the way, we pass a 3-D display about Saint Anne's life. It's not done with real sculptures—they're more like the dummies you see in store windows. Only these ones are wearing robes instead of tight-fitting jeans and sexy T-shirts that show their nipples.

Colette wants to stop at the display of old letters and back issues of *The Annals of Saint Anne*. *The Annals* is a magazine about miraculous healings.

"Only for a minute," I tell her when we're near the small dimly lit section that has rows and rows of letters and pages from *The Annals*. They're displayed along a wall inside glass cases and lit from behind.

When we were little, Colette and I always begged Mom to bring us here. Mom would read us the old letters. I think I still know some by heart. I try saying one in my head.

We placed a picture and a statue of Good Saint Anne underneath Gilles's pillow. Since then, Gilles has had no more convulsions.

Colette drags Iza over to one of the frames. She's going to read the letter out loud, the way Mom did. Even before I'm close enough to hear, I know which one it's going to be. Colette's favorite—from the achy bones lady.

Springfield, Massachusetts
April 1952
I am writing this letter to attest that after suffering for many years from severe arthritis and rheumatism, I was cured after a single application of Sainte Anne's oil. My bones no longer ache on rainy days.
Yours in the Lord,
Yvonne C. Desmarais

"You should get a copy of that letter for your shop," Iza tells us. "You could hang it up near the miracle oil."

"Hey, how come we never thought of that?" Colette's voice bounces off the walls.

"Shh," I tell her. "This is a place of worship."

"No, it's not. It's a museum."

"You're supposed to be quiet in museums too. Plus, it's a basilica museum."

Iza uses her elbows to separate us. "An-ette!" she says. "Quit arguing, will you? Besides, the lecture's about to start."

୫୭

Father Francoeur is doing a PowerPoint presentation about his work in the Liberian leper colony. At first, I can only look at him from the corner of my eye. I see his priest's collar peeping out from under his dark suit. When I try to look right at him, my face heats up. Colette said she knew all along I was crushing on Father Francoeur. She knew it even before I did.

We're sitting in folding chairs. Colette insists we sit up front. "So you can be near you-know-who," she says, winking in a way that makes me want to strangle her. Thank God no one else hears her!

I'm wearing Mom's old cowboy boots. I found them when I went down to the basement to look for the free weights. They were all in the same box, and when I tried the boots on, they fit perfectly. "Consider them yours," Mom said when I came upstairs wearing them. "They're too small on me. Besides, it's not as if I'd have much use for cowboy boots now. Did I ever love those boots when I was your age! I practically lived in those things. I saw a picture of them in *Seventeen* magazine and I phoned every shoe store in Quebec City till I found a pair. And now all these years later, cowboy boots are back in style."

I'd rather look at my boots than at photos of lepers. Their skin is splotchy and the women are topless, their dark breasts hanging from their chests like overripe fruit.

I prefer the photos of the Liberian landscape—the forests of rubber and mango trees, a bird with a bill so huge it looks like it belongs on a dinosaur, flying against a turquoise sky. I also like the photos of the marketplace where the villagers sell clay pots and tie-dyed fabric.

I wince when Father Francoeur shows us a photo of a little girl with leprosy. Two of her toes are missing. The girl is wearing a bright blue headscarf and looking right into the camera. Colette stares back at her without even flinching.

Later, everyone laughs at a photo of a chimpanzee stealing a bunch of bananas from a stall at the market. "That chimp is from Bossou," Father Francoeur explains, "but there are lots of them in Liberia."

After the presentation, Father Francoeur gives his talk and there's a question and answer period. He tells us he spent nearly five years in a Liberian town called Ganta and that he likes the term *Hansen's Disease* better than *leprosy*. In Ganta, there were more than seven hundred people with the disease.

"Wasn't it difficult to…be around those people?" a woman sitting behind us asks. From the way she wriggles her nose, you'd think she's worried she could catch leprosy from looking at Father Francoeur's photographs.

Father Francoeur's answer makes me admire him even more. "You're right," he says, "it was difficult, especially at first. Most of us aren't used to being around people who are different from us, or who are sick. But it didn't take me long to realize that people with Hansen's Disease are no different than the rest of us. They feel all the feelings we do...love"—I hope the others don't notice me gulp when he says that—"and hate and everything in between. They have hopes and dreams; they want to make beautiful things just like the rest of us do."

There's a cardboard box on the podium in front of Father Francoeur, and now he reaches into it the way a magician reaches into a black top hat. Only Father Francoeur pulls out a terracotta pot, not a rabbit. The pot has a wide brim and a delicate narrow base. "It's the pot you saw in one of the slides. Made by a woman named Mamawa. Mamawa had Hansen's Disease."

Colette is bouncing again. "Weren't you afraid you'd catch it?" she calls out, not bothering to raise her hand the way we're supposed to.

"Leprosy is less contagious than most people think. Like AIDS"—I wince again; Colette still has to go for an HIV/AIDS test—"it can only be transmitted through bodily fluids. So, no, I wasn't afraid I'd catch it. I didn't have time to feel afraid. There was too much work to do. While I was there, we built latrines, a community kitchen and a small church."

Iza raises her hand. "Do you think a person like me could go to Africa some day and do community work like you did?"

When Father Francoeur smiles, I wonder whether I should say I want to go to Africa too. Maybe what Father Francoeur said is true, and I'd stop noticing how bad the people in the colony look once I got to know them.

"But Iza, who'd blow-dry your hair in a leper colony?" Colette calls out, and everyone, even Father Francoeur, cracks up.

"Ani," Father Francoeur says when we're all standing up to leave, "if I could have a word with you."

Colette nudges me. "We'll wait outside," she says. At least she doesn't wink.

I hope Father Francoeur can't tell I'm trembling inside. It feels weird to be alone with him here.

I bet he's going to ask about Mom or maybe about Marco Leblanc. I prepare my answers: Mom's spirits are picking up; she even wants to start lifting weights the way Marco's been showing her. I'm not sure how much to tell him about Marco. Maybe because he's a priest,

Father Francoeur will be upset to know Marco's got a boyfriend.

"You seemed upset this evening, Ani," Father Francouer says. "I wonder if it's something I could help you with."

"I'm fine," I lie. There's no way I can tell him about my dreams.

"Okay then," he says, "but if you need to talk, I'm here. We're friends, aren't we, Ani?"

"I guess," I say.

Father Francoeur steps back to the podium, where his laptop is. "Ani"—I can feel him looking down at my legs—"those are your mom's boots, aren't they?"

"Uh-huh. I found them in a box in the basement."

"Ahh," he says, closing his eyes, "that explains it. Have I told you how much you look like she did then?"

"A lot of people say that."

Father Francoeur shuts his laptop. "Do you mind unplugging the power cord, Ani?"

Maybe it's because I'm not used to wearing cowboy boots, but when I reach over to unplug the cord, I end up tripping over it. Just as I'm falling, Father Francoeur rushes over and grabs my arm to break my fall. His fingers press into my arm. His hair is thick and dark. He smells like lemon soap.

I want to touch his hair. I want to kiss him. I lean in a little closer. I can see the pores on his chiseled nose.

Father Francoeur releases my arm. Then he takes a step back. Does he know what I was thinking?

"My God," I say, "I don't know what got into me. Forgive me, Father Francoeur."

He rubs the skin above his priest's collar. "There's nothing to forgive, Ani. Nothing at all."

But I know there nearly was.

Father Francoeur smiles. For a second, I'm afraid he's going to laugh at me. "It's those boots," he says. "They need new soles. Take it from me. I specialize in souls."

It's a bad pun, but we both laugh. The tension that was in the room is almost gone.

Though Father Francoeur hasn't said so and Mom didn't let on, I'm beginning to get something I didn't get before. Even if the clues were there. The little Bible Father Francoeur took to Liberia. Even the fact that Mom never mentioned him. "You and my mom—you were more than just friends, weren't you?"

"That was a lifetime ago."

He could have said they were just friends, but he didn't. So I was right. "Did you...you know...love her?"

"I did."

For a moment, I'm jealous of my own mom—and of what she had with Father Francoeur.

"So why'd you become a priest? Why didn't you marry her?" If he had, Father Francoeur might have been my dad. Only I wouldn't have been me. And Colette wouldn't have been Colette. Everything would have been different. And I wouldn't have had my dad.

Father Francoeur gestures to two folding chairs in the front row. I sit on one; he takes the other. He is too far away now for me to smell his soapy smell.

"It happened—my calling—after Marco's accident. I suppose it was because I felt responsible. Not only because I let Marco go home drunk. There was more to it than that."

I feel Father Francoeur's eyes on my face, as if he is trying to decide whether he can trust me with the rest of the story. I nod to show him he can.

"Marco's gay," Father Francoeur says. There's no judgment in his voice. "He told me so that night. I told Marco he could change. That what he was doing was a sin and that he had to stop or he'd go to hell." Father Francoeur's Adam's apple is quivering. It's as if a small bird is caught inside his throat.

"After the accident, the guilt was almost too much for me to bear. I shouldn't have left him alone. Not in the condition he was in." Father Francoeur pauses. "I even contemplated suicide. The only place that brought me peace was the basilica. I'd been brought up religious. And so I consecrated my life to God. And your mother... well, she understood. She let me go."

I wonder if in all my life I'll ever love someone enough to let him go.

Twenty-One

I still don't know if I believe. Not just in miracles, but in the whole package. Our Savior. Catholicism. Religion.

If it weren't for Catholicism, Father Francoeur might not have told Marco being gay was a sin—and Marco might not have drunk so much and got himself run over by a train. And if it weren't for Catholicism, women in Tante Hélène's time and even some Catholic women today might use birth control and not be forced to have so many babies.

As for miracles, Mom's lower body looks more shriveled every day. It's a miracle, I suppose, a small miracle, that at least she's working out with the weights I found in the basement.

I guess I always thought that as I got older, I'd understand things better. That I'd be able to decide about miracles and religion and the kind of person I want to be—a believer like Mom, a skeptic like Dad or something in between. But the older I get, the more confused I feel.

The weirdest thing is that despite the whirlpool swirling in my head, the thing I really want to do is go to confession. I can't even explain the urge to myself. Only that it has something to do with who I was before Mom's accident, and the peaceful feeling I still get when I'm inside the basilica. The kind of feeling that brought Father Francoeur comfort after Marco got run over by the train.

Forgive me, Father, for I have sinned. I practice the line in my head, though I've said it thousands of times. I started going to confession when I was in grade three. Back then, my biggest sin was pulling Colette's hair.

For the first time ever, it strikes me as kind of odd that I have to call everyone Father. God, the priests, Dad. It's like Catholics have too many fathers to keep track of.

There's a row of six confessionals to my right. Two have green lights over their doors, which means there's a priest inside ready to take confession. A red light over another one of the confessionals suddenly turns to green and I see Madame Dandurand pop out. I drop my head so I won't have to say hello. I wonder what she came to confess. She certainly doesn't look like the sinful type. "They're usually the worst," Dad would say. "Holy-moly on the outside, only not so pure inside." Now I see how maybe Dad's crack could apply to me too.

When the clicking sound of Madame Dandurand's high heels fades, I make a dash for the closest confessional. I don't want to run into any more people I know. The moment I push open the door, I know I've done the right thing. The musty smell is as familiar as an old friend. I can practically feel it opening its arms to take me in.

Luckily I'm not claustrophobic because the confessional is tiny, smaller even than one of those old-fashioned phone booths, the kind people used before everyone (except my dad) had cell phones.

Though I can't see his face, I already know the priest sitting on the other side of the grill is Father Lanctot. I knew it even before I stepped inside the confessional, because I heard him blow his nose. I'll bet he stuffed the used Kleenex back up his sleeve.

I don't know what I'd have done if it had been Father Francoeur on the other side of the grill. I could never have confessed to him—especially since part of what I have to confess is about him.

I take a deep breath as I sit down on the hard wooden stool inside the confessional. The stool is still warm from its last occupant. I wonder what he or she came to confess and whether Father Lanctot was shocked by what he heard, though I guess by now, Father Lanctot has heard it all.

This isn't going to be easy, but I know I'll feel better afterward. Sometimes, a person has to tell her story. Get it out, then start over again. Make a new beginning.

I flatten the sides of my skirt. "Forgive me, Father, for I have sinned." That's the easy part. It's like saying "Once upon a time" when you tell a fairy tale. Always the same. What comes next is going to be harder. I've done so many sinful things lately I hardly know where to begin.

"I don't feel compassion for sick or handicapped people—the way I should." I didn't plan to start with that; it just pops out.

I can only see the dark outline of Father Lanctot through the grill. He looks like a shadow of himself and now he's nodding. I guess he's heard that one before.

"My mother is handicapped, and I don't even feel much compassion for her." Though I've been speaking in a low voice, I drop it even more. Father Lanctot straightens his shoulders. Even though I can't see him, I can see his shadow. "I get grossed out when I see her legs. They just hang there, useless, like a rag doll's. Looking at them makes me feel sick."

I don't stop for air. I'm afraid if I do, it'll be too hard to get going again. "And I don't have compassion for my sister either. She's got ADHD." I wonder if Father Lanctot knows what that is. And I wonder how many other confessions he's listened to in his lifetime. Thousands probably. Maybe even tens of thousands.

"And I have…I mean I had…a crush on someone I shouldn't have had a crush on."

Father Lanctot's shadow is nodding again.

"He's a priest."

Father Lanctot's shadow goes still.

"Don't worry. It isn't you."

"I should hope not." Father Lanctot's voice is flatter than usual.

For a second, neither of us says anything.

"Is there more?" Father Lanctot asks me.

"I don't know whether I believe in—you know—Him. God."

"Doubting is part of faith."

"It is?"

"Certainly. True faith makes room for doubt."

I don't know how to tell him that I don't know what he's talking about. How can faith and doubt go together? I always thought they were opposites like hot and cold, or fire and water. Or my mom and my dad.

"You said you don't have much compassion for your mother. Correct?"

"Uh-huh." I can practically feel the guilt coming out of my pores.

"But that means you have some compassion. Correct?"

I hadn't thought of it that way. Maybe I've focused too much on what I'm missing and not enough on what I've got.

"You must draw on the compassion you have. Compassion is like a well. It goes deeper than you expect." I think about the old stone well behind the farmhouse on Côte Ste-Anne. When we were little, Dad used to lift us up so we could peer down into it. No matter how hard we tried, we could never see the bottom. "Now about that priest you say you have a crush on. Have those feelings passed?"

I wonder if Father Lanctot notices I've just squirmed in my seat. Maybe he's like a border guard—trained to watch for suspicious signs.

"Pretty much," I tell Father Lanctot.

"Pretty much is a good start," he says.

"Do you really think so?" This confession is turning into more of a conversation than I expected.

"I do."

"Then I guess I'll try to think of it that way. Pretty much is a good start," I say, trying out the words and the idea. "So what's my penance?"

"I was just getting to that. Why are all you young people always in such a rush?" Father Lanctot sighs. "I want you to say twelve Hail Mary's every night for a week. Is that clear?"

"Yes, Father."

"I absolve you from your sins in the name of the Father, the Son and the Holy Ghost."

"Thank you, Father."

"God be with you," Father Lanctot says. As I get up from my seat, I hear him blow his nose. When I leave the confessional, the light is flashing green again.

Twenty-Two

The first thing I see when I leave the basilica is another flashing light. This one's red and it's coming from the top of an ambulance pulling out of the basilica parking lot. At first, I think it's one of the pilgrims—someone has fallen out of a wheelchair or had a heart attack. Still, the wailing sound of the siren rattles me. For the rest of my life, that sound will always remind me of the day of Mom's accident and how I heard the siren in the background when Colette phoned to say something bad had happened. And how after that, everything in our lives changed.

I look over at the parking lot. Armand is there, wearing his orange vest. When he sees me, he waves, gesturing for me to come over.

"Did you hear what happened to the new priest?" he shouts as I walk toward him.

"D'you mean Father Fr-Francoeur?" My chest feels tight. What can have happened to Father Francoeur? Has he had a heart attack or some kind of stroke? Or was it an accident like Mom's? What I'm thinking most of all is, Haven't enough bad things happened to me already? Doesn't God grant some kind of immunity to kids whose moms are paralyzed below the waist? Can't He at least do a better job of looking after the people I've got left?

Armand nods yes. He means Father Francoeur. I rush over to Armand, grabbing hold of his elbow. A driver waiting for Armand to direct him to a parking spot honks. "What happened to him? Tell me!" My hands are shaking.

Armand signals for the driver to wait. "Take it easy, Ani," he says. "I heard Father Francoeur had an allergic reaction. He was having lunch in the clergy cafeteria and his throat starting closing up. The paramedics said he went into anaphylactic shock."

Armand turns around and directs the driver to a free spot. Then he walks back to where I'm waiting. "They think he might have an allergy to mangoes—because another priest told the paramedics they had mango yogurt for dessert."

"Mangoes?"

Armand must notice how upset I am, because he says, "I didn't know the two of you were so close."

"We are. I mean...we're not. He's a family friend. D'you think he going to be all right?"

"I'm sure he'll be fine. The paramedics were pretty pissed off he'd let his EpiPen expire. Look, Ani, you gotta chill out. Like you said, the guy's a family friend. It's not like he's your dad. Imagine if, after everything you've been through, something bad happened to your dad—or to Colette..."

"If you're trying to make me feel better, Armand, it's not working."

I can still hear Armand's words inside my head as I walk along Avenue Royale. *It's not like he's your dad.*

The window shade is already down at Saintly Souvenirs. But now I hear Colette's voice inside my head too. *He's old enough to be your father.*

That's when it occurs to me. What if—? *What if—?* No, there's no way, no way in the world...

Then again, it's possible. I try to do the math, but the numbers get jumbled inside my head like a calculator just before the battery dies.

I'm sixteen. How old was Mom when she had me? Why can't I remember? It must be because I'm trying too hard to figure it out.

Okay, I think I've got the numbers right now. It could be. It could, even if it's the grossest thing in all the world. The grossest thing ever.

Too gross to even think about. But there's the math—and now the mango allergy.

Lots of people have allergies to peanut butter. But allergies to pitted fruit are less common. What if it's not just a coincidence?

My head is going to explode. Or else I'm going to vomit. Maybe both at the same time.

There's a wooden bench up ahead. If I sit for a bit maybe my stomach will settle. Pilgrims walk by, but I don't notice them and they don't notice me. I need to talk to someone. Not Mom. No way. Not now, not when she's still so messed up. And definitely not Dad.

I'm thinking back on the conversation I overheard last week. Dad wanted to know something. What was it he said again? "I need to know who it was." Mom didn't want to tell him. She said he'd never needed to know before. Oh God, maybe that's what they were talking about. Maybe Dad has known all along I wasn't his. But Dad's my dad. I know he is.

It's hard to even hold up my head. When I close my eyes, I see myself sitting on a wooden bench on

Avenue Royale, my head slumped over. Why can't this be happening to someone else?

Thank God I didn't kiss him. Though I came close. Now I really want to vomit.

A girl about my age is trying to get by in her wheelchair. I bring my legs a little closer to my body to give her more room. In the past, I might have looked away. This time, I don't. She has freckles on her nose and stronger biceps than I've ever seen on a girl. She maneuvers the wheelchair past me.

When our eyes meet, she nods. There's nothing disgusting about her. Nothing at all. I'm the monster, not her. All along, I've had it wrong. The really monstrous things don't show on our outsides.

"Hey, Ani," a voice calls. At first, I think it's Iza. I don't want to talk to her. I'll tell her I have to get right home to look after Mom. I'll say I'll phone her later.

But it's not Iza; it's Colette. When I see her, the tension in my shoulders starts to loosen and the sick taste in my throat goes away. Colette drives me crazy, she has always driven me crazy, but she is always there. Like she is now.

Colette and Maxim have been to the clinic for the HIV/ AIDS tests. She's blurting this out on the sidewalk for the whole town to hear. "There's a new AIDS test," she's saying.

"People used to have to wait two weeks for results. But we'll know sooner. And the nurse, she's Tante Hélène's friend, she says she isn't too worried. Maxim's only had sex with two other girls. And he used a condom with the second one."

"Colette! Can you at least whisper?"

"Oops," she says, dropping her voice. "You're right. I guess this stuff is kinda private, isn't it?"

"Let's go somewhere quiet. I need to talk to you about something important."

"You do?" Colette's voice goes up, as if I've offered her a gift.

The Scala Santa is Colette's idea. She tells me how it's her and Maxim's favorite spot. She doesn't have to say for what; I can figure that one out on my own.

When Colette takes my arm, I feel a little less monstrous. "Did you know Mom used to smoke behind the Santa Scala?" I ask her.

"I'm not surprised," Colette says.

A woman is admiring a huge oil painting of Jesus on the cross. Some pilgrims are trudging up the stairs. One of them, a man, is on crutches and a younger person, probably his son, is helping him up.

Colette leads me up the stairs and around the building to a shady spot at the back. "There's a concrete ledge we can sit on," she says.

We hoist ourselves up onto the ledge. I let my legs dangle. Colette bangs her heels against the wall. We're close to Côte Gravel, the steep winding street that leads up to Côte Ste-Anne. We hear a car chug as it climbs Côte Gravel. But from where we are, we can't see it and it can't see us. This is the perfect hiding place.

No wonder Mom came here to blow smoke rings and to teach Father Francoeur to smoke. Now I wonder what else they did behind the Scala Santa. "The thing I need to talk to you about," I tell Colette, "it's pretty gross."

Colette has finally stopped kicking. "Did I do something wrong?"

"No, this is about me."

She raises her eyebrows. "You did something wrong?"

"Not really. Not me. It's more something Mom did." I pause. What I'm about to say is going to change everything between me and Colette. "With Father Francoeur. A long time ago."

"Oh," Colette says. Her pupils are getting big the way they did in my dream. "Do you really think—?"

"Uh-huh, I do." I take a deep breath before I go on. "I'm nearly sure that Father Francoeur's my dad...my biological dad." Saying it out loud makes me feel even more certain that it's true. And also a little bit afraid. There's no going backward now.

"Do you think Father Francoeur knows?" Colette asks.

"I'm not sure. But I think Dad does. I think he's known all along."

Colette has started kicking again. "You're probably right."

"Then he's not my dad. Not my real dad." I look at Colette. "And we're not real sisters." I can feel the tears roll down my cheeks.

When Colette wraps her arms around my shoulders, I let her. All our lives, I've had to look out for her. That's what being a big sister means. This time though, she comforts me, rocking me from side to side.

"You're wrong about that part," she whispers. "No matter what, Dad's your real dad—and we're real sisters."

"That's not true," I say between sobs. "You know it's not true."

"It is true. I know it here." When I pull away a little, I see Colette is tapping her chest exactly where her heart is. "So are you going to talk to her about it?"

"I don't think so. Not yet anyhow. And you better not either." I don't mean to sound so sharp.

Colette's kicking double-time now. "She should've told us."

"Yeah, she shouldn't have lied. Especially since she raised us not to lie," I say.

Colette looks at her feet. "It wasn't exactly a lie. Maybe she was waiting for the right time to tell. Or maybe the longer she waited, the harder it got."

"I guess. But still. She should've told us."

We just sit that like for a while: Colette kicking at the air, me with my legs dangling down. I think about the matchy-match sisters and I feel a little jealous of them. At least they know who they are to each other.

We're still sitting on the ledge when we hear the tinkling sound of a girl laughing. "Are you sure coming here is a good idea?" Her accent sounds Spanish.

"You're gonna love it." The words are followed by a laugh.

Colette and I both freeze. That voice. The laugh. Maxim.

A second later he's in front of us, holding hands with the dark-haired girl whose photo he took at the canyon. The one he spoke Spanish to.

Colette jumps to her feet. Her face looks like it's about to crack. "Maxim! What the hell? Why are you holding her hand?" She glares at the girl. "He's my boyfriend, bitch!"

The girl shakes her hand loose from Maxim's. Her dark eyes look angry. At who, I can't tell.

But she's not half as angry as Colette. "I hate you, Maxim! I really hate you!"

I'm standing now too. "Let's go," I say, trying to take hold of Colette's elbow. "Don't even talk to him. He's not worth it."

Maxim puts his hands in his pockets. "It's not like we're married or anything," he tells Colette.

"You could at least say you're sorry," I hiss at Maxim. Maybe he never learned how to apologize.

Colette is sobbing. The Spanish girl bites her lip. "I'm sorry," she tells Colette, but Colette won't look at her.

"We should go," Maxim tells the Spanish girl. "Listen, Colette," he says, looking back at her, "I'll phone you later and we'll talk, okay?"

Colette sniffles. I know her—she never stays mad. She's going to give Maxim another chance, and there's nothing I can do about it.

Colette rubs her eyes. When she speaks, her voice is shaky, but the words come out clear. "Don't bother," she tells Maxim. "We're done."

I decide not to say anything bad about Maxim, even though I want to. It won't help Colette if I do. She rests her head against my arm.

"I really hate him," she says, hiccupping, and then she starts to sob all over again. "But I love him too." Saying that makes her cry harder.

There's nothing for me to do but let Colette cry and hand her Kleenex when she needs it.

"There's only one good thing," Colette says when we finally get up from the ledge.

"What's that?" I expect Colette to say that, soon, Maxim is supposed to go back to Quebec City. Or maybe that she's glad that, thanks to her, the Spanish girl found out Maxim was a jerk before she fell for him too.

"The one good thing was you were here."

Twenty-Three

I make Colette swear she won't talk to Mom or Dad about Father Francoeur. "Not till I'm ready," I tell her. "And I'm not ready yet."

I guess I don't really have to worry since Colette has other things on her mind.

When we get home, she bursts into the house and heads straight for the blue velvet couch. "How could he do this to me?" she wails, crossing her hands over her chest as if to prevent her broken heart from popping right out.

Mom is more supportive than I expected. She makes tea and fusses over Colette. Maybe we've been so busy looking after Mom we haven't given her a chance to look

after us. "A bubble bath might help," she tells Colette—
and I can't help wondering if bubble baths helped Mom
get over Father Francoeur after he decided to become
a priest.

Being home is hard for me. It's as if the lighting has
grown darker. In the kitchen, the photograph on the
fridge door of Mom and Dad looks different now too.
Mom's smile looks forced. And in the living room, the
Jesuses on the crucifixes look more discouraged than
usual. As if they're having trouble bearing the weight of
all our sins.

Colette has taken Mom's advice and is having a
bubble bath. Mom has wheeled herself into the bathroom
to keep Colette company. "You don't have to talk about
it," I hear Mom say to Colette, "unless you want to."

Mom sure hasn't wanted to talk about her past.

My eyes land on a weight-lifting magazine by Mom's
side of the bed. Marco must have brought it. Because it's
not lying flat, I smooth it out. Which is when I realize
there's something under it. The miniature Bible Father
Francoeur returned to Mom. I pick it up and flip it open.
There's an inscription in Mom's handwriting. The letters
are so tiny, I need to bring the Bible to the front window
to read the inscription. *I understand*, it says. *Forever
your T.* The inscription is dated Easter 1993.

Forever your T. Easter 1993. Eight months before I was born.

She should have told me. She shouldn't have let me figure it out for myself like this. It isn't right. Especially since she raised us to always do the right thing. She even named me after a Saint! And in his own way, Dad's no better. He's been lying all this time too! Pretending to be someone he isn't. I wonder who else in town knows that Father Francoeur is my biological father. I don't think in all my life I've ever felt so angry and alone. Everyone I know has been trying to fool me. Every single one!

Iza's mom must know. She and Mom were superclose when they were growing up and when they first had kids. There's all these pictures of me and Iza in our Snugglies, our moms grinning at the camera.

"I'm going for a bike ride," I call out to Mom and Colette.

"Just be back in time for dinner," Mom calls back. "Your dad's planning something special."

My dad.

I stop to catch my breath as I bike up Côte Gravel. The narrow road snakes around until it reaches the top of the cliff.

I stop again when I reach the farmhouse on Côte Ste-Anne. When I look up, all I see is blue sky.

Iza and her family live in a mansion farther down the road. Dad says it's ridiculous for three people to live in such a big house.

The automatic sprinklers are on. I find a dry spot for my bike, then make a run for the front door. A pale, almost translucent rainbow appears over the jet of water from one of the sprinklers.

Iza's doorbell chimes like a church bell.

"Ani," Lise says as she opens the door. "It's lovely to see you, honey, but I'm afraid Iza's at work."

"I'm not here to see Iza."

"You're not?" Lise shows me into the huge living room. Though she's home alone, she's got lipstick on. I sometimes wonder how she and Mom could ever have been such good friends.

We sit down on a gigantic beige sofa. "How's your mom?" Lise asks. "I keep meaning to come by. It's just that things have been crazy here."

It's hard to imagine things ever being crazy in this house. Everything is in its place, right down to the crystal candy dish on the coffee table.

"Mom's started lifting weights. Marco's been showing her how."

Lise wrinkles her nose as though she just smelled something sour. "I didn't think they were still friends."

"They weren't—until lately." I wonder if Lise can tell what I'm thinking—that lately she hasn't been much of a friend to Mom either.

"So, Ani, what is it you want to talk to me about?"

My mouth feels suddenly dry. "Is it okay if I have one?" I say, eyeing the oval mints in the candy dish.

"Oh those, they're just for show," Lise says, popping up from the sofa. "How about some juice?"

"A glass of water would be good."

I take a long sip of the water Lise brings me, but the dry feeling in my mouth doesn't go away. The water is the fizzy kind and Lise has put a slice of lemon on the edge of the glass. I guess it's for show too.

"I've got some questions," I tell her.

"What kinds of questions?" Lise folds her hands neatly in her lap.

"About my mom and Emil Francoeur. And about me."

Lise turns to the window. When she turns back to face me, I notice how her face has none of the lines Mom's face does.

"Ani, honey, I think you need to have this conversation with your mom." Lise's voice is very gentle. But her lips are pursed together. She knows something.

"I can't talk to my mom about this stuff. Not now. She's still too messed up."

Lise looks down at her legs, folded neatly at the ankles. She is wearing a pair of crisp beige slacks. "I know I'd be messed up if it was me. But I always thought your mom's faith would get her through any crisis."

I'd always figured Mom and Lise had grown apart because Lise is obsessed with having the perfect life and Mom's more real. But now I wonder if God got in the way of their friendship too.

"Can't you tell me anything?" I ask Lise.

Lise shakes her head. "There's just one thing I can tell you, Ani. One really important thing: Your mom and dad love you very much. And they're special people. Both of them."

But that's all she'll tell me.

છ૭

Colette is still convalescing—taking long bubble baths and writing madly in a journal Dad bought for her—but getting a little better too. The first few days, she didn't even want to leave the house. Mom and Dad let her skip two days' work at the store.

Today Colette wants to know if, after we close up the shop, I'll bike over with her to Tante Hélène's. To pick up some nerve tonic Tante Hélène made for Mom.

"Are you sure going over there's a good idea?" I don't say Maxim's name since Colette tears up when she hears it.

When Colette sucks in her breath, I know it's because she's still suffering. That even if I think Maxim was a jerk and she's better off without him, she really did care for him. "He won't be there," she says. "I checked."

We make a quick stop at Tante Hélène's. "You and I are always going to be friends, aren't we?" Tante Hélène says, patting Colette's shoulder and giving her a big hug before we go. Colette nods.

On the bike ride back, Colette insists on stopping at the small cemetery on Avenue Royale. Because it's not far from our house, we used to come here a lot when we were little. Someone has put a pot of yellow pansies on one of the graves. We sit on a bench under a giant weeping willow tree. Colette kicks at the bottom of the bench with her heel. I try not to let it bother me.

"How's your heart?" I ask Colette.

"Still broken," she says. "He texted me to say he wants another chance." I can tell she's watching for my reaction.

"Don't—" I stop myself. Colette has to figure this out for herself. "What are you going to do?"

"I'm still thinking about it. I don't know if I trust him. I think he likes girls too much. Tante Hélène says her husband had the same problem and that she gave him too many chances. How's your heart?" Colette asks me.

"Confused."

"I guess you haven't talked to Mom yet."

"Not yet. But soon. And hey, thanks for not blurting anything out," I tell her. "That can't be easy for you."

Colette looks insulted. "I said I wouldn't." Colette stares up at the willow. I look up at it too. It makes a giant silver-green umbrella.

"I'm pretty sure I'm right," I tell Colette.

She knows what I mean. "You do look like him."

"I do?"

"Uh-huh. Little things mostly. The thick hair and you both have those really long fingers." Colette slides her hand over mine. It's true. Her fingers are shorter and thicker than mine. "You laugh the same too."

"But don't you think it's…you know, gross?"

Colette is tapping the bench now. Maybe she thinks better when some part of her is moving. "No," she says, "it's not gross. It just is."

"But I wanted to kiss him." My voice breaks when I tell her this. It's the part I'm most ashamed of.

"That was before you knew." Colette gives me a sideways look. "You didn't kiss him, did you?"

"No, I didn't. But I wanted to. Oh, Colette, I feel so ashamed."

"You don't have anything to be ashamed about." Colette says this as if the matter is settled.

Twenty-Four

I t's only four days till Saint Anne's feast day on Sunday—and the pilgrims are taking over our town. There's about twenty times as many pilgrims as residents. And by Sunday, there will be thousands more. We're being invaded.

It happens every year, but somehow I'm still not used to it. There are people everywhere, many of them on crutches or in wheelchairs; long lineups outside L'Église, at Sweet Heaven and at the Blessings Office; people posing for photographs on the basilica grounds; traffic jams at every corner. They jabber to each other in languages I recognize—French, German, Spanish, Cantonese and Russian—and some that I don't. Armand and Maxim are working overtime in the parking lot. There needs to be at least two of us in the store at all times. But there are benefits to having your town invaded: like all the other businesses on Avenue Royale, we'll earn more this week than in all the other fifty-one combined.

I haven't had much time to think—and maybe that's okay. I'm still not ready to talk to Mom or Dad or Father Francoeur. Besides, what would I say? Dad, you're not my dad. Father Francoeur, in case you haven't already figured it out, congratulations, you're a father. No, I feel like I need to let things sit a while longer, the way I do after I've had a big meal. My brain is digesting. The other thing I've been doing is watching: looking for signs, for differences. Does Dad treat Colette better than me? Is he more patient with her? Does he love her more? Does he laugh harder when she says something funny? But though I've been watching carefully, like a scientist peering through his microscope, I haven't noticed anything different. Dad's worried about Mom, but otherwise, he's the way he always is. Kind and steady.

This morning he's sprinkled icing sugar in the shape of a smile over our French toast and made eyes from chocolate chips, the way he used to when we were little. Colette bursts out laughing when Dad serves her. Mom smiles too. I think the weight lifting is doing her good.

She's wearing a white sleeveless blouse, and I can see that her upper arms are getting some definition. More importantly, she's not as down as she was before she started training with Marco.

We're talking about how busy the store has been when Dad comes up with the idea that Colette and I should have a day off. "We're going to need the two of you in the store from tomorrow through Sunday pretty much nonstop. Clara is working today, and I can go in to help. You two can have the day to yourselves—to get out and get some fresh air."

"But who'll look after Mom?" Colette and I ask at the same time.

"I don't need constant looking after," Mom says.

"We could go to the canyon. And Mom, you can come with us!" Colette says.

I watch for Mom's reaction. Colette shouldn't have said that. She's just reminding Mom of all the things she can't do anymore. Colette should've checked with Dad and me before bursting out with the idea.

Only Mom doesn't look upset at all. "I'd love to feel the spray from the waterfall on my face," she says, lifting her face up toward the ceiling fan that's rotating over our dining-room table. "It's been forever since I was at the canyon."

Of course, we all know it hasn't really been forever. The last time Mom was at the canyon was the day of her accident.

"It's settled then," Dad says. "I'll give the three of you a lift over. You can phone when you're ready to be picked up."

"Can I invite Tante Hélène too? I think she's getting lonely with Maxim working so many hours this week," Colette says. We all look at her when she says Maxim's name. Her eyes don't tear up this time.

Dad takes another bite of French toast and wipes his mouth with his napkin. "That's one of the things I love about you, Colette, the way you're always thinking about other people."

Colette is already in the kitchen, phoning Tante Hélène. I wonder what things Dad loves about me.

ॐ

We can't take the wheelchair on the suspension bridges, but we can take it on the bigger paths. Colette pushes the wheelchair, but I don't entirely trust her. What if something—a butterfly or some cute guy—distracts her and she lets go when we're hiking downhill? I walk alongside Mom.

We get as close as we can to the waterfall. There's a clearing up ahead with an old picnic table. I help Colette park Mom's wheelchair at the narrow end. This way, Mom will feel the spray from the waterfall on her face.

I hadn't realized what good friends Colette and Tante Hélène have become. Colette recognizes native herbs and plants without Tante Hélène having to tell her what they are. Today, Tante Hélène, who is wearing her floppy hat again, has brought along a burlap bag to collect plant samples. She's also brought lunch. Whoever heard of a tofu sandwich? It turns out to be better than it sounds. "Tante Hélène marinates the tofu in soy sauce and cilantro before baking it," Colette explains.

"And why do I have the feeling the cilantro comes from Tante Hélène's herb garden?" Mom says.

"It certainly does," Tante Hélène tells her. "You know, Thérèse, I could help you start a herb garden of your own. Colette says there's a sunny spot behind your kitchen."

Mom doesn't say yes, but she doesn't say no either.

"I think I'll get some fresh air," Tante Hélène announces after we've finished eating. "Colette, are you coming?"

"But there's air everywhere here," Mom says.

I catch Tante Hélène and Colette exchanging a look. Ahh, I think, they want to give me some time alone with Mom. Only I'm not sure I want to be alone with her. I need for Colette to be here too. After all, what I need to talk to Mom about involves Colette too.

"Colette, can you stay?" I ask her.

Tante Hélène adjusts the brim on her sunhat. "I'll be off for a little while then," she says.

It's hard to know how to start this conversation. "Mom, there's some stuff I need to ask you about." "Mom, who's my real father?" "Mom, I'm losing my mind and you've got to help me."

"Maybe you're not in the mood to talk today," is what I end up saying. It sounds like I'm protecting Mom, but really I'm protecting myself.

Mom pats my forearm. "Let me decide that for myself, Ani," she says. She folds her hands in her lap. "So, girls, what is it you want to talk about?"

Colette looks from Mom to me. I know Colette must be dying to ask Mom about my real father, but she's holding back. She knows I have to be the one to ask. "About me," I say. "And about you and Father Francoeur."

Mom's face gets pale, and for a moment, I'm afraid she's going to faint.

Her eyes have that glazed look they had after the accident. "I didn't know you knew," she whispers. It's as if
Mom's afraid the grass and trees will hear her.

"Look, Mom," I say, my voice almost as low as hers,
"you don't have to tell us. Not if it's going to make you
sad. Or upset."

Colette can't keep it in any longer. "You do too have
to tell us," she snaps. "We're old enough. You've kept the
truth from us too long already. Besides"—Colette throws
her hands up into the air—"the whole town knows."

Mom presses her elbows down on the arms of her
wheelchair. "You're right. You should have known by
now. It's just…well…the time was never right. Maybe it
never is when you've got something hard to do." Now she
reaches out across the picnic table, taking my hand in one
of hers and Colette's in the other.

"I suppose I'd better start at the beginning." Mom
turns to look right at me. "Emil was my first love. I think
I loved him even in grade two. When we were teenagers,
it seemed natural for us to be together. He was my best
friend and my lover." I feel my cheeks get hot when Mom
says this, but she doesn't seem at all embarrassed. All these
years, I thought Mom was too shy to talk about sex. Now
I think maybe it was her way of keeping her past a secret.

"We should have been more careful, but then if we had been, I wouldn't have had you." Mom squeezes my hand really hard when she says this. "Beautiful, wonderful you."

Beautiful, wonderful me. I feel like I need to take in Mom's words and keep them somewhere close—so I can remember them when I feel lost or overwhelmed or ashamed.

"Emil came from a religious family," Mom continues. "Two of his uncles were priests, a cousin on his mother's side was a nun. Then after Marco's accident, Emil became even more religious. I think it was because he felt responsible—that he shouldn't have left Marco out on the street, drunk."

Mom shakes her head at the memory. I can tell she's wishing things had been different. But if they had been, what would have happened to us? Father Francoeur might have been my father after all, but then what about Dad? And Colette? Even if Colette sometimes drives me crazy, I can't imagine life without her in it. Maybe that's what being sisters means.

"I'd just found out I was pregnant when Emil told me he'd decided to enroll in seminary school and that he wanted to become a priest. Lise thought I should try to talk him out of it. That I should have told him I was pregnant. But I couldn't do it. I thought there was no higher calling than to devote your life to God. There was no way I could interfere with that."

Mom smiles a little at the memory. I can tell that even after so many years, Mom still thinks she did the right thing.

"What about Grandmaman and Grandpapa? What did they think?" I ask her. I can't remember much about Mom's parents, who died when Colette and I were little. Only that Grandmaman laughed a lot, and that Grandpapa had a silver tooth.

"For as long as I could, I didn't tell anyone but Lise. My parents—well, when they finally found out, they were upset, of course. But I wasn't the first girl this had ever happened to—and they loved babies. I'm sure there was gossip, but mostly the people in town were good too. Some of them must have known about Emil and me, but they never said anything. Not to me anyway. And they all turned up when you were born—with presents for you."

"You must have felt awful after Emil left," Colette says. I know she's thinking about Maxim.

"It was hard, especially at first, but I knew I'd done the right thing. And then"—Mom is smiling now—"your father came along." I expect Mom to look only at Colette when she says that, but Mom doesn't. She's looking at both of us. She's saying that Dad is my father too.

"Tell us what he was like. Tell us why you fell in love with him," Colette says.

"Well, at first, he made me laugh. Which was what I needed. And once I started to show, well, I had to tell him. He never judged me. And he told me that he loved me—and the baby I was carrying. His goodness won me over. Though I'm afraid that lately I haven't appreciated that part of him enough. You know what Lise used to say? She said your father was the real saint in our town!"

"Dad, a saint?" Colette thinks that's funny. "But you forgot to say he's handsome too!"

"Yes, he's handsome too. But that was a bonus."

"Does he know about Emil?" I ask.

Mom sighs. "I finally told him. Last night."

For a while, none of us says a word. Not even Colette. It's as if we're all listening to the sounds of the breeze, the rushing water, and someone—maybe Tante Hélène—humming in the distance.

"What did Dad say?" I ask. There, I've done it. I called him Dad. It wasn't so hard.

Mom's folds her hands and makes a steeple with her pointer fingers. This time, she looks up at just me. "He said it didn't make a whit of difference. None at all."

Twenty-Five

Today isn't only Saint Anne's feast day, it's Ste-Anne-de-Beaupré's day too. Today, Ste-Anne-de-Beaupré is in all her glory. Our town is glowing like a bride on her wedding day.

I have never in all my life seen so many people. Monsieur Dandurand says it's because of the economy. "People these days are more desperate than ever for miracles," I overheard him tell Dad last night, when we ran into him on Avenue Royale.

It's impossible to get anywhere quickly. The sidewalks and streets are thronged with people. They're mostly pilgrims who've come to pray for their loved ones or themselves, but there are gawkers too. People who've come to watch us celebrate. When they're in our store, they turn over the Jesus statues to see where they are made. Gawkers hardly ever buy anything.

Because the town is so busy, Mom and I leave extra early for Mass. I have to weave her wheelchair through the thick crowds on the sidewalk. When I finally get inside the basilica, park her wheelchair at the end of our aisle and sit down on the pew, I take a deep breath. The Dandurands turn to wave at us; Mom and I wave back. With so many strangers in town, it's as if there's a new solidarity between the locals. We've all been invaded.

There isn't room for all the people who've come to attend Mass today. Many are clustered by the TV monitors; others are standing at the back of the basilica near the confessionals, their hands folded in front of them, their heads slightly bowed.

Mom is wearing a new dress she ordered online; it's the same pale blue as her eyes—my eyes too—and it has sheer sleeves that are an even paler blue. She's resting one hand on my knee. Father Lanctot is leading the Mass, but today, half a dozen other priests from around the province have come to join him. They are standing together behind Father Lanctot, near the altar. Father Francoeur is there. He is the tallest and most handsome. I try to see myself in him. He is too far away for me to see the long fingers

Colette says I inherited from him. It feels so strange to know this man is my biological father.

The choir's singing sounds like birds and bells. I inhale the familiar scent of musty wood and incense. Father Lanctot reaches into the sleeve underneath his cassock for his Kleenex, blows his nose and stuffs the handkerchief back up his sleeve. "May God be with you," he says.

"And also with you," we respond.

"Today is a day of great celebration and great holiness in our little town of Ste-Anne-de-Beaupré," Father Lanctot says. Though I've heard the story of Saint Anne many times, I don't mind hearing it again. Especially today. Father Lanctot tells us about Saint Anne's parents, Stolan and Emerentiana. If Colette were here, she'd make a joke about those names. I can practically hear her whisper: "That poor Emerentiana. Boy, she musta got teased on the school bus. Let's hope her parents called her Emmie for short."

"Stolan and Emerentiana were an exemplary couple," Father Lanctot says, taking his time over every word, "who educated their daughter in the love of God and neighbor." That gets me thinking about Mom and Dad. I wonder if Father Lanctot suspects the truth, and if he does, whether he thinks Mom and Dad are exemplary too. And when Father Lanctot mentions neighbors, I picture Marco, who was out on his balcony, lifting weights, when Mom and I were leaving for Mass. I noticed his boyfriend's car was parked outside and I felt glad for Marco.

When he is done with the story of Saint Anne, Father Lanctot reaches into his sleeve for his Kleenex and blows his nose again. "And now," he says, peering up at the congregation with his watery eyes, "I'm going to ask Father Francoeur to say a few words. Father Francoeur was raised in Ste-Anne-de-Beaupré and it's here that he found his calling. But he spent more than fifteen years in Africa, working in a leper colony, where he helped establish a church and a small school. And we've recently learned that Father Francoeur will be returning to Africa to resume this important work."

I feel Mom's hand go limp on my knee.

My own heart is beating double-time underneath my blouse. How can Father Francoeur be leaving? He may not even know that I'm his daughter. It isn't right.

I'm shaking inside as I watch Father Francoeur take his spot at the microphone, next to Father Lanctot. Father Francoeur nods to the congregation. He doesn't seem nervous at all, not even in front of so many people. And then for a split second, he looks right at me and Mom. Mom is smiling too hard. She does that when she's trying not to cry.

"Saint Anne taught us to believe in miracles," Father Francoeur says, and again I'm struck by his voice, the way I was that time when he drove me home from the hospital. How calm he sounds, how safe his voice makes me feel. Even though he's standing right here, I feel already how much I'll miss him when he returns to Africa. "Displayed right here in this basilica, you'll see crutches and walking sticks and prostheses that pilgrims left here after they prayed to good Saint Anne and were miraculously healed. Across the parking lot, in the basilica museum, you can read letters from pilgrims whose prayers were answered by Saint Anne. All of those events were miracles.

"But today, I want to talk to you about another kind of miracle. The kind of miracle that is perhaps somewhat less dramatic, but that is nonetheless a miracle. And that's the miracle of faith. It's here today. In this basilica. At this very moment. I can feel it. And you can feel it."

Father Francoeur pauses. I know it's because he wants us all to feel the miracle he is talking about—the miracle of faith. And despite everything my family has been through, I can feel it. It's a kind of energy, a soulfulness that's in the air, filling the spaces between us and the golden ceiling that towers overhead. But the energy isn't coming from some mysterious place up high; it's coming from all of us.

From every person in the basilica today. Even from the gawkers. And that, I decide, is because somewhere in all of us, there is faith. Faith that life makes sense. Faith that even though terrible things happen, there is still goodness and hope.

Now I remember Father Lanctot's words in the confessional: "True faith makes room for doubt." If Father Lanctot is right, then there is room for all my doubts and all my questions.

I reach for Mom's hand and squeeze it hard. She squeezes back. I know what she's telling me. That she has not given up.

For me, the outdoor ceremony that comes afterward is the highlight of Saint Anne's feast day. A small group of specially selected ill or handicapped people gets to take part—and this year, Mom is one of them. Father Lanctot himself called her last week to invite her.

So after Mass, Mom and I wait by the confessionals until nearly everyone else has left. We form a line with the others who have been invited to participate. One is a boy my age, who must have cerebral palsy and is also confined to a wheelchair. The boy's face looks like it is frozen in a permanent grimace. He's with his dad, and I let them go before us.

I wheel Mom down the exit ramp next to the main stairs. As I look out at the basilica grounds, all I see are people. Some have brought their own folding chairs; most are standing.

The late morning sun lands on Father Lanctot's bald spot. In the bright light, I can see how lined his face is, and I wonder how long it will be before he is too old to conduct the Mass on Saint Anne's feast day.

A microphone has been set up outside and when Father Lanctot goes over to it, the entire town seems to fall silent. Even the crows understand that this is no time for cawing.

Father Lanctot says a few words in Latin. And then, one by one, he blesses each person grouped in the circle around him. I watch his face as he looks at the grimacing boy. All I can see in Father Lanctot's eyes is kindness. The boy's eyes glisten with pride.

Now it's Mom's turn. Father Lanctot kisses her forehead. "In the name of Saint Anne," he says, "I bless you and pray for your healing—both physical and spiritual."

I remember back to when Mom was released from hospital and how she insisted on coming to pray at the Miraculous Statue. Looking back, it seems silly that I ever thought for even a second that Mom might be miraculously healed just from saying a prayer. I must have been crazy.

I'm more realistic now. I don't need to look at the boy's grimacing face or at Mom's useless legs to know that neither of them—or any of the others in this circle—are going to be miraculously healed. None of them are going to be adding their crutches to the collection on the church walls, or abandoning their wheelchairs. But right now, at least, that feels okay.

Maybe it's because I know what's going to happen next. The part of Saint Anne's feast day ceremonies I love best.

I look up at the dozens of rectangular windows at the top of the basilica. From where I am standing, the windows look tiny, though I know they're not.

Mom is looking up too. I rest my hand on her shoulder, which feels more muscular than it used to.

And then, these windows—dozens and dozens of them—which are never opened except on Saint Anne's feast day, burst open all at once. Behind the windows, I can just make out the priests in white robes who've opened the windows.

And then—my favorite, favorite part.

The doves.

Each priest releases a single white dove.

Father Lanctot's voice crackles through the microphone. "By choosing to die for our sins, Christ has allowed each of us to be saved. Like these birds, we too can rise above our earthly cares and fly into heaven."

The doves—there must be thirty of them—soar away, and my heart soars with them. For just that moment, as the doves take off and disappear into the vast blueness of the sky, I'm a believer.

Twenty-Six

The afternoon goes by in a whir. Kind of like the doves flying off, only faster.

When it's finally over, and Colette and I are closing down the shop, I can't remember anything specific. Not the face of a single customer—there were too many. Not a single thing they bought—though I know we sold postcards and key chains and license plates and statues and Jesus-and-Mary salad spoons. All I remember is the *dr-ring dr-ring* of our old cash register and the bell on the shop door tinkling as new customers poured in and others streamed out.

"We must have made thousands!" Colette is saying. "I'll bet this was our biggest day ever!"

I want to tell her we don't know that yet for sure, that we still have to add up all the sales, but I stop myself. What's the point of spoiling Colette's fun?

Though the souvenir stores are closed for the day, Ste-Anne-de-Beaupré is still celebrating. I hope Sweet Heaven won't run out of Quebec maple fudge.

"I'm sorry you can't come to the parade," I tell Mom over dinner. Dad has made filets of sole with a *beurre blanc* sauce that he serves in a gravy dish that belonged to his great-grandmother. Mom closes her eyes when she takes the first bite of fish. It is good—light and moist—and the sauce tastes, well, buttery.

I don't think in all her life Mom has ever missed a Saint Anne's feast day parade, probably because the parade combines two of Mom's favorite things: religion and exercise. On the night of Saint Anne's feast day, thousands of pilgrims trek up the hill across from the basilica, past the stations of the cross, which are bronze statues that tell the story of how Jesus suffered for us. Because the hill is steep, it's a tough trek, and some people get so winded they turn back.

"I've made my peace with it," Mom says. "Besides, you'll go for me, won't you, Ani?"

"Of course, I will."

"And I will too," Dad announces.

"You will?" the three of us say at once, and then we all laugh.

Dad reaches across the table for Mom's hand. "I want to be able to tell you all about it afterward," he tells her. There's not even a hint of sarcasm in his voice. Colette and I look at each other. Next thing we know, Dad'll be asking Mom why we don't have a crucifix hanging in the dining room.

"You're my darling," Mom tells Dad.

Dad looks so pleased I'm afraid he'll burst.

I can't remember the last time I was out alone with Dad. "I know all these pilgrims are good for business, but to be honest, Ani," he tells me as we thread our way through the crowds on Avenue Royale, "I can't wait for them to all clear out of town. So life can get back to normal."

We're both quiet after he says that. Maybe it's because we're thinking the same thing: that after what's happened to Mom, our lives will never get back to normal. Maybe we'll have to settle for a new normal.

Up ahead, the hill shimmers with yellow lights. From where we are, the lights look like fireflies, but we know they're coming from the lanterns. Everyone in the parade gets a paper lantern with a little yellow votive candle flickering inside.

When we reach the base of the hill, Dad and I line up for our lanterns. There's a chill in the air I haven't felt all summer. When I shiver, Dad puts his arm around me. "Do you want my jacket?" he asks, starting to loosen his jacket from his shoulders.

"No, no, I'm fine."

"Look, Ani," Dad says, "your mom told me you know about us—and you." Dad is looking me in the eye. When he blinks, I know how hard this is for him. "I just need you to know one thing." He pauses. "It never made any difference to me. You've always been my daughter. Always will be." Dad's voice cracks when he says that.

"Excuse us," some pilgrims behind us call out. They're carrying a banner made from an old sheet with a huge drawing of Saint Anne on it. Saint Anne is wearing a long blue dress and someone has spray-painted a golden halo over her head. Dad and I move over to the edge of the path and wait there in single file as the pilgrims squeeze past us with their banner.

The man handing out lanterns gives us ours. "I know," I tell Dad. And because I know what he is really trying to say is that he loves me, I add, "I love you too, Dad. I just wish you'd told me sooner."

"Me too," Dad says. "It just never seemed like the right time. I should've been braver."

The first station is just a few meters up from the road. We join the crowd of people standing in front of the larger-than-life bronze Jesus being condemned to death. His face looks peaceful. Someone has left a bouquet of plastic red and white dollar-store carnations at Jesus' feet.

Dad is next to me and I can feel him shift from one foot to the other. All this religious stuff must be making him squirm. Dad rests his hand on my shoulder. "I need you to know too, Ani," he whispers, "that I won't be upset if you want to get to know him." At first, I think Dad's talking about Jesus, but then I realize he means Father Francoeur.

Maybe Dad hasn't heard that Father Francoeur is going back to Africa. Though I guess with email and Skype, I could still get to know him even if he'll be living on another continent. Only I'm not sure yet what I want from Father Francoeur. "I'll see," I tell Dad.

We follow the path past the next couple of stations, stopping only briefly to look at the bronze sculptures, but when we get to the fourth station, where Jesus is meeting his afflicted mother, Dad is out of breath. I hand him the plastic bottle I've brought along, and he takes a long swig of water.

Jesus' hands are stretched out toward Mary. Mother and Son gaze into each other's eyes. Even though they are bronze statues, I can feel they understand each other.

Mary understands what Jesus has decided to do; He understands how difficult it is for her to let Him go. Maybe that's what love is—caring so deeply about someone else that you can feel what it's like to be that person.

A pilgrim has looped a rosary over one of Jesus' long fingers. The colored beads glimmer under the light of our lanterns.

"You ready, Ani?" Dad asks. I guess he's had about all the religion he can handle.

I take Dad's hand. I'm getting a little winded now too. There's a stone bench up ahead, but three old ladies are sitting on it and another three are standing nearby, waiting for a turn to rest their legs.

Up ahead, the path winds like a corkscrew. It's thick with pilgrims, and when I turn my head, I see even more pilgrims behind us. Dad turns to look too. The yellow lights from the lanterns wink at us. It's as if there are stars on the ground instead of the sky.

Dad shakes his head. "I have to admit it's pretty. Maybe I shouldn't have said no all those years when your Mom wanted me to come with her."

"She's glad you came tonight," I tell him.

People are slowing down now and some pilgrims, especially the ones who are old or out of shape, are stopping to rest or have water.

From where we are now, we can see to the top of the hill. A crowd has gathered at the eleventh station. Here, Jesus is being nailed to the cross. I can't help shivering when I look at the bronze nails piercing through His wrists and knees. Better to look at His face. I study it, searching for some sign of panic or anger, but I don't see any. None at all. Just acceptance. Let it be. I don't know how Jesus did it. I know I could never accept that kind of pain—no matter how much I believed.

I can't stop looking at Jesus' face. He looks so...so human. Could that mean that sometimes even He had doubts and questions, not just about religion, but also about Himself? The way I do?

Dad has gone to wait at the edge of the path. I can feel him looking at me looking at the statue.

When I'm done, I slip my hand into Dad's. Together, we trudge to the top of the hill. The exercise has warmed me up. I stop, but only for a moment, at the last station: Jesus is being laid in the sepulchre. At last, His suffering is over. What's left is His story, and for believers, His example. I'm still not sure if I believe any of it.

Dad and I join the crowd of pilgrims filing down the road that heads back down to Avenue Royale. "I wonder if it's true," I say, looking over my shoulder at the hill.

Dad doesn't say anything at first. I know it's because he's thinking. "I suppose it could be," he finally says. Because the road is steep, we need to take small steps and lean back a little on our ankles. "Sometimes," Dad says, "a good story is as important as the truth."

The downstairs light is on when we get home. Mom's in her wheelchair, parked near the front window. "How was it?" she asks when we get in. At first, I don't know why she's whispering, but then I see that Colette has fallen asleep on Mom and Dad's bed. She's curled up in snail position.

"Better than I expected," Dad says. He puts his arm around Colette so he can bring her upstairs. She makes a little moaning sound, and Dad kisses her forehead.

Mom wheels herself over to me. She pats the edge of the bed, which means she wants me to sit there. My legs are still warm from the climb and sitting feels good. "So tell me all about it." If Mom's sad she missed the parade, I can't tell from her voice or her eyes.

As I tell Mom about the lanterns and the crowds and how even Dad had a good time, I notice her bite down hard on her lower lip. Something must be hurting.

I jump up from the bed. "What's wrong, Mom? Tell me what's wrong."

I must've raised my voice because Dad comes clattering down the stairs. "What's going on?"

We're both watching Mom's face.

She's gripping the sides of her wheelchair so hard her hands are shaking. "I've got some bad cramping," she says. She looks up at both of us. Her pale blue eyes look silver. "In my thighs."

Twenty-Seven

I t's too soon to get excited, but the neurologist in Quebec City thinks the cramps in Mom's thighs are a hopeful sign.

Hopeful. That's something I haven't felt in a while.

Marco can tell something's up at our house. When he comes by to help Mom with her weight-training routine, his eyes dart from her to me and back again. "Something feels different in here today. Lighter," he says.

Mom's eyes have a little of their old sparkle back—and for a moment, I'm afraid the cramping may not be anything more than some random thing, and not a sign that she is regaining sensation below the waist.

"I've been feeling some pain. In my thighs," Mom tells Marco. She says this in a quiet voice, and I wonder if it's because, like me, she is worried about how Marco will take the news.

I know if it was me and I'd spent more than half my life trapped in a wheelchair, it'd piss me off if some woman who's only been paralyzed for less than two months suddenly shows a sign—even a little one—that she might recover. I'd feel like it just wasn't fair, that the woman should take a number and wait her turn and that she'd be way behind me—twenty years behind me—in the recovery sweepstakes. I don't think I could stand the unfairness of it all.

But Marco doesn't seem pissed off. He wheels his chair next to Mom's. "Thérèse," he says, pumping his hand on her back, "that's great. Show me where you feel the cramping."

When she shows him the spots on her thighs, I expect Marco to look down at his own useless legs—that's what I'd do—but he doesn't. I think he's really happy for Mom. Too happy to think about his own troubles.

I ask Marco about it later when I'm helping him down the ramp from our house. "Is it hard for you? The news about Mom, I mean."

Marco looks me straight in the eye. "That's not the kind of question I expect from you, Ani. It's more of a Colette question."

He's right, but I feel like I know Marco well enough now to ask it. Maybe what he just said is his way of not answering. But a minute or so later, he says, "Sure I wish it was me, but you know what, Ani? I've had twenty years to make peace with being paraplegic. It took a long time, but I did it. And I can still be happy for your mom. For all of you."

Marco doesn't look anything like the bronze Jesuses at the stations of the cross. Those Jesuses don't have slicked-back, dyed black hair or bulging biceps or skin that's gone leathery from too much sun. But even so, right now, I'm remembering the look on the bronze Jesus' face when he was first condemned to death.

There's something Marco still wants to say. I know because he's watching me. "Besides," he says, "I've got something of my own to celebrate."

I wonder if Marco and his boyfriend are getting married, but that's not what it turns out to be.

"A guy I know is opening a gym on Avenue Royale, not far from your shop. He's offered me a job, working with disabled people. I told him yes."

"You did? That's amazing!"

"I know what you're thinking—that I'm not exactly a people person," Marco says.

"I wasn't thinking that. You're good with people. When you want to be."

"D'you really think so?"

"Uh-huh, I really do."

I'm starting to get better at hugging people in wheelchairs.

৪৩

The pilgrims have mostly cleared out of town. I can see the sidewalk again, and without all the cars, the air smells crisper. On my way to the basilica, I spot a porcupine crossing Avenue Royale. He's fat and funny-looking, with brown spikes, and I'm sure he's been hiding in the woods the last couple of weeks, waiting till now to cross to the other side of the street.

There's no line outside the Blessings Office. No pilgrims waiting with statues, nobody with a new puppy.

Emil…Father Francoeur…Father—I still don't know what to call him—is sitting behind the desk, scratching his temple with the flat end of a ballpoint pen.

He looks glad to see me. "Ani," he says, getting up from his chair, "I was hoping you'd come by."

"I didn't bring a toaster for you to bless."

The sound of Father Francoeur's chuckle fills the little room. Do I really laugh like him?

"Have a seat." Like always, I can feel him looking at my hair and eyes. I know that when he sees me, he is remembering Mom.

Father Francoeur sits back down in his chair and gestures for me to take the seat across from him. "So are you missing the pilgrims?" he asks me.

"Not really. They brought us a ton of business this year, that's for sure, though. But now, well, it feels like I can breathe again. Or almost, anyway."

Father Francoeur's eyes seem to darken. "You're not having trouble breathing, are you?"

The way he asks makes me wonder if he's figured things out. If he knows I'm his. "I'm allergic to mangoes," I tell him. It isn't what I planned to say.

"Just like me," he says, pulling his chair a little closer to the desk and extending his hands along the desk until they're only a few inches from mine.

"It's kind of an unusual allergy," I say.

"I know."

"It can run in families."

"I've heard that too."

I slide my hands off the desk and fold my arms over my chest. Father Francoeur's face is very serious.

"In a way," I tell him, "I wish you'd never come back to town."

I expect Father Francoeur to look hurt, but he doesn't. When he nods, I know it's because he's feeling bad for me. He's imagining what's going on inside me, and for a moment, I try imagining what's going on inside of him.

I uncross my arms. "I always thought I knew who I was, but now everything's different. From the first time I saw you, I felt there was something between us. Something familiar. And then that day at the museum—after your talk—I got confused." This part is hard to talk about, but I know I have to do it. I have to make things right. Not for Mom, not even for Father Francoeur, but for me. "I guess I needed to feel close to you. Only I didn't understand why. I didn't know that you were my fa—" At first, I stumble over the word.

"Father." We say it together, without stumbling.

I put my hands back on the edge of the desk. Father Francoeur reaches all the way over and lays his hands over mine. Colette was right. We have the same long fingers.

"Your parents came to see me last week to fill me in on"—I can tell from how slowly Father Francoeur is speaking that he wants every word to be the right one—"who we are to each other. Like you, I felt a connection the moment I saw you. I thought it was because you look so much like your mom used to. But then, Ani, I started realizing it was something else. A heart connection I'd never felt before. Something quite different of course from the feelings I had for your mother. And then... and then...I didn't dare to hope that you were mine."

"I am yours," I tell him. "Biologically, I mean."

Father Francoeur nods. "I understand what you're telling me. That you have a father. A real father who's been there for you all your life. But perhaps, when you're ready, you could make some room for me too?"

"Aren't you going back to Africa?" My voice quivers when I say Africa. Part of me wants Father Francoeur to go away so I can pretend I never met him; the other part wishes he would never leave.

"I fly out next week. But I may be back before Christmas—depending on how things go."

"You mean in Liberia?"

Father Francoeur looks down at his hands, which are still over mine. "No," he says, looking back up at me.

"Not in Liberia. Depending on how things go here. With you. On how you feel. On whether or not you can handle having me around."

"What if I don't know yet?"

Father Francoeur squeezes my hands. "I can live with that."

Twenty-Eight

C olette and I are both lying on our beds, reading.
I'm reading *The Life of Saint Anne*, only this
time, I've got a pencil in my hand so I can scribble notes
to myself in the margins. Such as, *Didn't Saint Anne
want to kill her parents when they dropped her off at the
church so they could keep their promise to consecrate her
to the Lord?*

Colette's got her nose inside an *US Weekly* magazine.
It's Saturday night and Mom and Dad are out on a date—
their second one since Mom's accident. Mom's been
getting a little more cramping in her thighs. The doctors
are "cautiously optimistic" and they've recommended she
step up her workout routine. They've given her exercises

for her legs and so the three of us have been taking turns helping her do leg lifts.

Marco's convinced the weight training made a difference. He wants Mom to write a testimonial he can hang on the wall at his friend's gym. Tante Hélène says it was her nerve tonic. Father Francoeur says it's God's plan.

Hope's a funny thing. A little hope can go a long way, and yet, there's something painful about hope too. If what we're hoping for doesn't happen, we might end up feeling even worse than we already did when the accident first happened. And yet the hope that Mom might regain some movement in her lower body has lightened the atmosphere in our house, just like Marco said. Hope is making us kinder with each other and more patient.

And that's when I realize that maybe it's true that the real miracle isn't when someone throws away their crutches or stops being paralyzed. Maybe the real miracle is way simpler than that. Maybe the miracle is not giving up. Maybe it's staying hopeful even when you're not sure how things will turn out.

Which may be why, even though I am concentrating on *The Life of Saint Anne* when Colette puts down her magazine and says, "So I was thinking…," I don't get upset with her.

I rest my book on my lap, using my pencil for a bookmark.

"Uh-huh," I say to Colette.

"I was thinking maybe I'll be a nurse."

"That's a great idea," I tell her. "Except you'll have to wear those hideous white nurses' shoes—with the rubber soles." Then I remember how good Colette has been with Mom and how she was the first one to get Mom to wash her hair. "I think you'd make a really good nurse."

"But what about my ADHD?"

I think in all the time we've known about Colette's ADHD, this is the first time she's ever mentioned it and it occurs to me now that Colette's ADHD isn't only a burden for all of us who know her, it's a burden for Colette too. A way heavier burden than it is for the rest of us. And yet, Colette never complains about it.

"You know," I tell Colette, "there could be a plus side to having ADHD—benefits that could come in handy if you're a nurse. Nurses need a ton of energy and they need to be able to bop around from one task to another. Check a patient's blood pressure, help them do leg lifts, change their bedpan."

"Uck, that part's gross," Colette says. She picks up her magazine. "Even with the bedpans, I think I still want to be a nurse," she says.

Maybe it's because Colette has told me her dream that I feel like telling her mine. "I want to be a historian," I tell her. "And the first thing I want to study is the real story of Saint Anne. I'm researching it now."

Colette kicks at her blanket so that one of her feet pokes out. "What do you mean by real story?" she wants to know.

"Not just the goody-goody stuff. How perfect she was, what a good daughter, what a good person and all that. I want to know how she felt when she was in a terrible mood, when she had mean thoughts, when she questioned everything—even God. And I want to know about her bad dreams."

Colette sighs from behind her magazine. "I'd read it," she says, "and not just because we're sisters."

Acknowledgments

Special thanks to Pat Norris for reading the first draft of this book; to Vincent DiMarco for his careful reading of the second draft and for his insights and useful suggestions; and to Elisabeth Klerks for responding to medical questions while we were both hanging out laundry.

Thanks also to Dr. Thanh Nguyen and to Anita Simondi for answering more medical questions; to Monique Lamarche and the welcome team at the Sainte-Anne-de-Beaupré Basilica; and to my dad, Maximilien Polak, for his careful reading of this book and for responding from his heart. Thanks to Katherine Walsh for her clever suggestion, and to Ryan Sheehan for helping me understand how miracles work. Thanks to Elaine Kalman Naves for her professional and personal support, and to Viva Singer for letting me talk another story out. Thanks to the many people I met on my visits to Sainte-Anne-de-Beaupré for sharing their town with me. Thanks to the Canada Council of the Arts for their support and for believing in this project. More thanks to the team at Orca, and especially to my editor, Sarah Harvey, for giving me the push I needed on this story. And, as always, thanks to my husband Mike Shenker and my daughter Alicia. I love you both.

Miracleville is *Monique Polak*'s twelfth novel
for young adults. Her historical novel, *What World is
Left*, won the 2009 Quebec Writers' Federation Prize
for Children's and Young Adult Literature. Monique
teaches English and Humanities at Marianapolis College
in Montreal and works as a freelance journalist. She
lives in Montreal with her husband, a newspaperman.
She believes in miracles.